When You Least Expect It

Also by Jennifer Friess

The Wind Could Blow a Bug

When You Least Expect It

The Riley Sisters

Book 2

By Jennifer Friess

Mr. Ugly-Man Entertainment
Adrian, Michigan

Mr. Ugly-Man Entertainment
Adrian, Michigan
First Edition June 2015
Text copyright ©2015 by Jennifer Friess
All Rights Reserved, including the right of reproduction in whole or in part in any form.
To book an event or to purchase additional copies, please visit:
imnotstalkingyou.com

ISBN 9780692452165

To Dave, my furry daughter, my dingo, always.

defaults

I've got a major
system
Internal
malfunction
Man the bridge
restore the defaults
it is not too late
not now
not if we can reach
operational
status again
restore the defaults
I can get back online
to a life that should have been mine
restore the defaults
I can be brave when before I was shy
I will learn to be tough & lie
restore the defaults
let me do it again

I just know I can't go on now
I've wandered too far away
from where I started
gone too far off course
restore the defaults
then I can see
where I quit being a person
and started being just me
--JLF 10/10/01

1

KILEY

Kiley gazed out the windows into the darkness as she autographed her novel for the last customer in the bookstore. She signed it, then smiled at the customer as she was hurriedly ushered out the door by the owner, Mrs. Bethany.

"Five minutes till close," she barked.

Kiley got the feeling that Mrs. Bethany didn't hold a lot of book signings in her store. But Kiley's agent seemed to be able to get her into almost anywhere: expos, libraries, bookstores—chains and independents. This didn't always make for a warm welcome, but Kiley was always grateful for anywhere she could get more sales and talk to readers, having one-on-one interaction. Her agent was happy that Kiley was so game to be on the road for long periods of time, traveling around the country. Most authors had 9 to 5 jobs and kids and obligations they were reluctant to leave behind. Knowing that tomorrow would be the end of seven months on the road, Kiley now realized maybe she should have been skeptical about why she was the only one willing to do this rigorous touring. Maybe there was a good reason why sane authors didn't want to.

Kiley got up and began loading the leftover books onto the metal cart the owner had pulled up next to the table where she had been signing. Mrs. Bethany would place one or two copies back on the shelf, no doubt returning the rest of the stock back to the publisher. Kiley gazed at the cover of her book. The picture featured a good looking man and woman in an embrace. But what always jumped out at her was her name. Even though it had now been a year since the book had first been published, she still felt like she was dreaming when she saw her name in print on the cover of an actual honest-to-goodness book.

Well, it wasn't exactly her name. It was her pen name, K. Riley, because her given name, Kiley Riley, sounded like a Dr. Seuss character. She couldn't use her middle name of Renee. Ick. Every Renee she had ever known was a bitch. It was kind of cool being known as an initial. It also doubled as an actual name, "Kay."

She flipped the book over in her hands and looked at the picture of herself on the back cover. The team at the publishing house had wanted her to change her hair, have it look more natural for the picture, but she had resisted and finally won out. No one seemed to be a big fan of the sleek black bob with bangs she had sported since high school, but she loved it. And it was HER hair. No one else should get a vote.

Most people are pretty impressed when they find out that her first book was published while she was still attending Alva University for her bachelor's degree. Well, her only published book, so far. If she was honest with herself, she was impressed by this too.

Kiley had done writings that were so much more serious. Started stories that she spent years working on, only to abandon them. She never thought the little free-write she started at 1:00AM about her jacked up life at the beginning of her sophomore year of college would turn into a novel. It only took her three weeks to flesh out the first draft. By the end of sophomore year, Kiley's favorite English teacher had read it and was helping her to find agents to shop the novel to. It took months before a publisher bought it. It made her a bit disillusioned by the whole process. It wasn't the romantic experience she had always dreamed that it would be. Writing was the fun part. And she tried hard to remember that through everything that came after. There was another year of going through the editing process. Ugh! She could barely recognize the finished product as her story. The publisher paid her, and slapped her name on the center of the cover, so they must have thought it was still Kiley's work.

Kiley received her box of advance reader copies on Christmas Eve, her senior year. There was no doubt that everyone received a copy as their Christmas gift. Although, in retrospect, she probably shouldn't have given copies to her parents. But Kiley didn't want to think about all that family drama right now. That January, it was available for purchase. While the publisher let Kiley postpone a real publicity tour until after her final classes ended in May, she still did occasional newspaper and radio interviews to support the book. She multitasked and did these while completing her classwork. It was a good thing she had planned ahead and completed her senior research project the first semester, rather than waiting till the second. Actually, Kiley had to give credit to her big sister Jane for that advice. Jane was always the planner in the family.

She didn't get to go on any big, national TV shows. But she did get to do local morning shows and talk shows. The first time she was super-nervous. But once she learned the TV lingo and what camera to look at, she was as good as gold. There was one appearance she had to fly to, but most she would just drive herself to. If they were on a weekend, sometimes her boyfriend Ted would come along.

He would say, "Let's pretend this is a little mini vacation."

She would say, "It IS a little mini vacation."

But he never liked this clarification, for some reason.

Ted wasn't scheduled to graduate until December. He said that was why he didn't mind traveling with her sometimes. All his toughest classes he would be taking in the fall. Ted was a biology major. His plan was to go on and get his master's degree. He made fun of Kiley when she had first tried to secure an agent for her story. He had thought she was crazy and had delusions of fame. He fed her statistics of how many writers actually supported themselves solely from their craft. Ted was a glass half empty kind of guy.

Of course, they weren't yet dating at that time. Ted just lived in the same dorm as Kiley. They often saw each other coming and going. They passed each other at the mailboxes and ran into each other in the laundry room. They started dating, well, sometime around when the publisher gave her a deal.

Wait, was that right?

He had asked her out. She had been so flattered, that of course she said yes. They had been a couple ever since.

Ted was the same height as Kiley when he had shoes on, which made him shorter than a lot of other guys. He was skinny. If he forgot to eat lunch, he could be classified as scrawny. He had beady eyes that saw the world through metal-rimmed glasses, which sat atop his nose that didn't quite fit into his face. He wasn't classically handsome, but he had a kind of dork-sheik about him.

Once she had finished her classes, she took off for her official book signing tour across the country. Kiley's agent helped her to set up appearances. She even skipped graduation to go. She had the registrar ship her degree to her mother. Why bother with a ceremony symbolizing the start of her life, when she could already be living it?

It was discouraging, at first, when so few people would show up for her book signings. It wasn't at all like she had pictured when she daydreamed about becoming a writer. She had imagined being in a big, national chain bookstore with the smell of coffee in the air, and a line of people curving all the way out the door and around the building. But with only two large national bookstore chains remaining, most of her stops were in small, independent bookstores that became cramped when you added an extra table and chairs.

The publisher kept stressing to her how important it was for an unknown author to get out and meet people, to get her name (and book) in front them. They said it was the same as with a new band needing to tour. While it was great having strangers tell her how much they enjoyed reading her book, it seemed everyone always asked the same question:

How did you come up with the idea for your story?

The answer Kiley always gave was that it was based on her own life, which truthfully, large parts of it were. But the truth, which she never told them, was that it had come to her in a dream. But she couldn't tell people that. It sounded so— Stephenie Meyer. She desperately wanted people to believe she was a good writer, not just a transcriber of dreams. She wanted to have wonderful ideas of her own freewill, not from her subconscious. It seemed like the lazy man's way to create a story.

She felt more comfortable the more signings she did. Ted came with her for a month in the summer, to keep her company. But a little part of her was happy when he went back to school for the fall semester. She was lonelier now, with no one else in her hotel at night to talk to. But when Ted was with her, she always seemed like she had to put on an act to keep him happy. Like if he saw her pick coleslaw out of her teeth with her black, plastic spork, he might be repulsed and run screaming the other way. She felt like Ted held her to a higher standard than she held herself. And that was kind of annoying.

She snuck in visits to her mom and dad when she could. She talked to her identical twin sister Miley several nights a week on the phone. Miley always said she couldn't be on a six month trip like that. She just wasn't programmed for it. Kiley liked traveling and seeing different cities and towns. But she was still lonely. She was becoming too used to this transient life. She needed to get back to reality. And start a second book already! Her future standard of living depended on it.

After the books were all on the cart, Kiley grabbed the other assorted odds and ends from the table. She dropped her empty cup of fountain coke and the crumpled napkin containing the crumbs from her orange cranberry muffin into the garbage can. She picked up her selection of Sharpie markers she had brought, black and silver, fine and ultra-fine point, and put them back into her messenger bag. Just then her cell began to ring. A quick glance at the picture on the screen told her it was her older sister Jane.

"Hi. I'm not interrupting, am I?" Jane asked worriedly.

"No. Perfect timing. I am just about to walk out the door," Kiley replied.

She covered the mouthpiece of the phone and thanked Mrs. Bethany for having her. She only grunted in reply, although by most book signing standards, Kiley's little book had done very well for her business tonight. Kiley waved at the two employees in the back of the store who had helped with set up, then pushed her way out the glass door with the metal frame. The little bell chimed in farewell.

"I just wanted to make sure you are still planning on arriving tomorrow," Jane inquired.

"Yes. I would love to just come straight down now, but I'm in Arkansas," Kiley said, approaching her white SUV that glowed under the parking lot lights. Climbing behind the steering wheel of her Toyota RAV4, she watched as the owner locked the door and flipped the sign to "Closed." "I am pretty sure I would fall asleep on the way to Alabama."

"Oh, that is fine. I would rather not have to worry about you falling asleep and ending up dead in a ditch tonight."

"Ah, I miss you, optimistic sister," she replied, sarcasm dripping from every word.

"Very funny. Do you think you will make it here by dinnertime tomorrow?"

"That is my plan."

"I can't wait to see you."

"I can't wait to see you, too. I bet you have changed a lot in the three months since I saw you last. Time to head to the motel."

"Goodbye."

"Bye."

Kiley drove toward the nearest interstate, where she had seen a bunch of chain motels, and a few mom and pop joints that looked like they could be a set for a new horror movie. Coming into town, she especially remembered seeing one that looked like it had recently had a fire, in the last five years or so, with boards covering the windows. But there was a giant brand new shiny banner hanging across that building which read "Now Open for Business." Kiley couldn't imagine anyone dense enough to actually stop there to get a room for the night. She was terrified to even drive past the place, afraid that a ghost would come up her tailpipe, or in through her ventilation system, and possess her.

She checked in to a low-budget but reasonably clean-looking motel. She handed over her debit card at the front counter, praying that there was enough money remaining in her checking account for both a room tonight and gas tomorrow. She pulled her little carry-on case to her room, swiped the key card, turned on the light, then fell face first onto the bed. Kiley was so tired. She wished she was still a little kid and could just sleep like this. Her appearance clothes would get wrinkled, but she wouldn't be having any engagements in Oakley and could have them dry-cleaned before any future ones. But sleeping in her dress clothes wouldn't be very comfortable.

Kiley pushed herself up off the bed. She pulled an old, stretched gray T-shirt out of her suitcase. She didn't bother to look for her own toothbrush. She opened the one sealed in plastic wrap provided by the motel instead. Then she laid down on the lumpy mattress. She tried to fluff the flat pillow, but it was no use. The low thread count sheets scratched her as she tossed and turned. She hadn't paid a high enough price for this motel for them to have a budget big enough to use fabric softener. She turned on the television to her favorite late-night talk show, hosted by Timmy Killon. The radiating glow of the screen and incessant drone of the men talking soon lulled her into sleep.

2

Kiley used to like driving, but now she was just sick of it. She wanted to get to her destination and not have to start her SUV again for at least a week. The sun was sinking lower in the darkening sky. She was only an hour out. Being on South 223, headed toward Oakley, she could already feel her body relaxing. She was headed home. Well, to her hometown anyway. The house she had grown up in with her parents and her sisters had been sold after their divorce when she was 15. Kiley and Miley, along with their mother, Helen Riley, had moved in with their Aunt Jamie in Huntington. That is where they had finished high school. Her dad had gone to take care of his ailing mother in Jackson, until her death a few years later. He must have put down roots, because he stayed. Kiley's older sister Jane had gone off to college. Miley and Kiley's relationship with Jane actually improved once their parents were removed from the situation. But she wasn't going to think about all that fucked up shit just now. Jane was the reason Kiley would be in Oakley by dinnertime.

Kiley could see the large farming complex in the distance; all of the grain elevators, bins, barns, garages, and the office that made up the business of Tucker Farms. The fields stretched out on either side of the road. Freshly planted distinct rows of winter crops gave the optical illusion of bending as they reached toward the horizon with the motion of the moving vehicle. Kiley knew it was the right homestead, because there was no other farm this big anywhere nearby. She could just make out the chipped paint of the wedding proposal for Jane that her now-husband Wade had painted on one of the silos. She pulled into the driveway of the Tuckers' large farmhouse. It is a good thing it was large, because right now there were seven people living in it, and there were about to be two more.

Kiley parked her car behind one of the pickup trucks, not knowing where would be a good place to not block someone. Kiley was used to parking for the night in a parking lot. She was going to be staying here awhile, at least a few weeks, but some things were just not as clear cut as they would be at an impersonal hotel.

She stepped out of the car and slammed the driver's door. Somewhere from within the house she heard a dog bark. She opened the rear tailgate and slid out her big suitcase. It hit the ground with an unceremonious thud. As she stood it up and pulled up the handle, she heard plodding footsteps approaching on the gravel.

"Oh my God. It is so great to see you!" Jane yelled as she came closer to hug Kiley. Jane's light brown hair was up in its usual ponytail. Kiley had once read somewhere that how people wore their hair in high school is how they would most likely wear it for the rest of their lives. That would be true of her older sister. Jane had always favored comfort over style. Her current physical state wasn't going to change that anytime soon. Jane's blue eyes beamed at the sight of Kiley.

"Wow. It is great to see ALL of you, too!" Kiley exclaimed. Jane and Kiley hugged awkwardly around Jane's giant, round belly.

"What did you expect? I'm almost nine months pregnant!" Jane said, sarcastically.

"Well, I guess when you put it that way, you COULD be bigger," Kiley appraised her sister's baby bump. Kiley had not seen Jane in months. "I am so glad you didn't have it before I got here."

"I haven't had any contractions or anything, so we will see. They may have to go in after the little sucker," Jane pondered, putting her hand on her belly affectionately. "I am so glad you came to be my nanny."

"I wouldn't go that far," Kiley's eyes bugged out a little, "but I will help where I can."

Wade, who had followed Jane out, came around to grab Kiley's large suitcase. Wade and Jane had been married for two and a half years. Evan Tucker, Wade's father, grabbed Kiley's carry-on bag out of the car. Mr. Tucker owned the house and the farm.

"Any more bags, Kiley?" Mr. Tucker asked.

"Um, in the passenger side. And please don't judge me by the cleanliness of my car, Mr. Tucker. I have been living in it for six months," she yelled, as he made his way around the vehicle.

"Please, call me Evan," he replied.

It was throwing Kiley off, having people help her carry things. All the cheap motels she stayed at she schlepped her bags around herself. This was the first indication that after being on her own for four years, it might be hard to reacclimate to a family environment.

"C'mon. Dinner's almost ready," Jane led them into the house. It was kind of silly, as she was slowing everyone down with her weighted pace.

"Did Donna cook it?" Kiley asked, hopefully.

"Of course. You deserve a good, old-fashioned home-cooked meal. There is no better cook in these parts than my wife," Evan boasted. He was always happy to brag about his wife's cooking.

A haze of smoke surged out the door as Jane opened it. Walking in the door, the smell of homemade fried chicken reached Kiley's nostrils. The aroma of grease hung heavy in the air. Her nose told her that burnt stray buttermilk batter bits in the pan had overcooked and were the source of the kitchen smog. Kiley thought she might pass out from the overpoweringly delicious aroma. She had only had Donna's cooking on a few occasions, one of which being Jane's wedding rehearsal dinner, but it never disappointed.

Kiley followed Jane through the door. A large, orange dog leisurely wagged its tail as Jane approached. When it got a whiff of Kiley's unfamiliar sent, the dog went into a crazy barking fit. Kiley liked dogs, but was a little afraid of all the teeth she saw as the dog growled at her.

"Dave, come," a man called from the living room. The dog barked three more times at her, the hair on his back standing at attention, before turning tail and heading further into the house to obey his master.

Huge hooks filled with coats hung on the wall just inside the door. There was a striped rug over the tile on the entryway floor. It could hardly be seen under the pile of boots and shoes that eclipsed it, mostly men's. Many were covered with a reddish-brown crust. Kiley was going to hope that it was only dirt. She figured Donna must make them all remove their footwear here. It was the only way that the carpet in the house would ever survive to see another year. There was a door to Kiley's left that seemed to go directly into the kitchen. There was a short hallway to the right. There were at least three more doors down there. The living room lay straight ahead, filled with bodies. She found herself smiling reflexively at the smell from the food, even though she was entering a room full of people who were virtually strangers.

"Hi Kiley."

"Welcome."

The room collectively greeted her as she came in. She knew all the guys were Wade's brothers. She used to know all their names, but was now fuzzy on who was who. She had met so many new people in the past year. The unknown female must be one of their wives. Jane led Kiley through the living room and in front of the pass-through window for the kitchen, where Donna spotted her.

"Oh, there you are! Give me a hug, honey." Donna embraced Kiley in a giant hug before she ever had the chance to protest. Not that she would have. Donna was pleasantly plump with a wild nest of curly burnt sienna hair. Kiley didn't know her well, but Donna was the most genuinely nice person she had ever encountered.

"Sorry about the smoke. Happens every time I make fried chicken," Donna paused, taking a breath. "Are you excited to become a first-time aunt? Cuz I am SO excited to become a step-grandma-in-law, or whatever!"

"Yes, I guess so. I am interested to see how Jane does with labor," Kiley said.

Jane held up a middle finger for her sister that no one else could see as she had already snuck into the kitchen.

"Oh, honey. I wanted to tell you what a great book you wrote. Oh, but I bet everyone tells you that. I read it cover to cover. Everyone in town is so proud of you..." Donna could talk a mile a minute, and use more exclamations than anyone could believe possible. Kiley was out of breath just listening to her.

"But one thing did bother me about the book. I never realized Jane was so mean to you growing up."

"It's not Jane!"

"It's not me!"

Kiley and Jane yelled in unison.

That is one thing that Kiley never anticipated would be such a big deal about her book. The main character had an evil older adopted sister. The older sister character was in no way based on Jane, other than maybe that she was adopted. But now everyone thought Jane had been a wicked step sister. Even their mom had called Kiley and Jane to see if there was any truth in the writing to real life.

"Oh, well, that's good. We are so glad you could come stay for the birth of the bouncing baby and for the holidays. It will be so good for Jane to have family around at this time."

"You are all my family," Jane said to Donna loud enough for those in the living room to hear, but Donna pretended not to notice. Maybe the statement had embarrassed her. Jane snatched a biscuit off the counter behind Donna's back and took a bite out of it.

"Thanks for having me. I know you already have a full house. But it will be so nice for me to be off the road for a while," Kiley sighed. 'That is an understatement,' she thought to herself.

"Hey, people can only check-in if they have a definite departure date," a loud guy yelled from the couch in the living room.

"Then you are more in violation of that rule than anyone else here!" a younger-looking guy said. Everyone laughed.

Kiley wasn't used to spending copious amounts of time with loud men. Ted definitely didn't qualify as a loud man, and he wasn't into horseplay or games. He was too serious for that. Kiley had grown up in a house full of girls. Her own father had been the quiet type. She would have to stay close to Wade and Jane for protection. On second thought, Wade often seemed a likely target. Kiley would have to hide behind the pregnant woman.

"C'mon everyone, gather round the table. Dinner is ready," Donna sang. Literally, the words came out like a song.

"It's been ready for forty-five minutes. We were just waiting for that chick to show up."

"Shut up, Josh."

Kiley saw the youngest brother jab his elbow into his older brother Josh's ribs.

3

JOSH

Josh tried to get a good look at the new arrival as they all shuffled around the table to their chairs. She hung back until Jane led her to an empty spot at the table. Josh had already forgotten which sister this was... Kiley? Miley? Why did their names all have to rhyme?

All they needed was another woman in the house. He could barely remember now what it had been like when his mom had been here. For more than a decade, it had just been his dad, him, and his three brothers. Then his dad had remarried. Donna was nice enough, but then in her wake followed two more females. Now this one. If the new baby came out a girl, the whole balance in the house would be shifted to pink. It was almost more than a guy could stand.

Josh remembered Kiley vaguely from Wade and Jane's wedding. Who could forget that jet black short haircut with the bangs that she always sports? She never lets it grow past her chin. It left an impression. Mostly, he decided, it made her look like she was trying to be a bad ass that she wasn't.

But that wedding was three years ago now. She would have still just been a teenager then. Women were enough of a handful. Josh wasn't looking to raise any himself up from goofy teenagers.

Although, he definitely found something attractive about her now. She had a tight little body. The T-shirt and jeans she wore were all rumpled from her trip here from god-knows-where. A large hole halfway down the right leg let her knee hang out. They had, after all, pretty much ripped her out of her car and drug her in the house so they could all eat. Hell, he would have done it himself, but no one else probably would have looked at it as a kindly gesture. When they did it, somehow it was "hospitality." But, man, he would love to get her out of those clothes, maybe a shower to get her wet, then mmm...

Shit. He couldn't let himself think like that now. Not when he had an actual plan for his life. Goals! He couldn't be dickin' around with every hot little number he saw. He had to keep his eye on the prize. Work a lot of hours, save a lot of money. Plus, he had size in his favor, but he was pretty sure if he screwed around with Jane's little sister, Jane knew the spots that would inflict the most pain if she got angry with him.

KILEY

Kiley tried to follow the many conversations happening around the dinner table, but soon failed. She talked to Jane for quite a while, but then Jane had to get up to use the bathroom. Apparently pregnancy had that effect on people. Kiley could not believe how much food her usually dainty sister was packing away. That had to be way more than eating for two. Maybe she was having twins and no one had thought to tell Kiley.

In Jane's absence, Kiley sat quietly and tried to put a name to each face. There was Evan Tucker, obviously, the father. Having grown up in this town, she of course knew him. His family farming business is pretty much what kept the town afloat. He helped to store, sell, and distribute other farmer's grain to market, as well as his own. Evan was like the town hero. He was also its most attractive father, although in the seven years since she had lived in this town, his once black hair was now about fifty percent black and fifty percent gray. He was in his mid-fifties. His eyebrows were only just starting to do that out-of-control bushy old man thing. His body was fit in an aging way.

Donna sat beside him. She was actually Evan's second wife. His first wife, and mother of all his sons, had died tragically in some way before Kiley could remember her; probably cancer. It seemed silly to ask now, when it had been almost 20 years ago.

Donna was only five foot five, which added to her round appearance. She was eleven years younger than her husband. She had curly brown hair with flex of red. It always looked as though she tried to keep it short, but she had forgotten several months of hair appointments and it had gotten away from her. But her hair had looked like that for years, so it must actually be her intended style. Donna and Jane had first met as co-workers at the Diner. One of only two restaurants in town, it had been destroyed by a tornado when Kiley was still in high school. It had since been rebuilt. Jane had always had a strong friendship with Donna that Kiley had often been jealous of. Being in this house and seeing them behave as mother and daughter rekindled this resentment, although she knew it should not. Were they not all adults now?

Josh sat next to Donna. That must make Josh the second oldest. The oldest Tucker son had his own home with his wife and kids nearby. Kiley remembered that Josh, and Wade who sat next to him, were only a year apart in age. That must make them 31 and 30. But no one would know that by looking at them. Wade looked like a male model. He had always been the only son with light blond hair, which he kept a little longer on top and very short on the sides. He had blue bedroom eyes, and always had a great body. Kiley had been so proud when her big sister had nabbed the best looking guy in town for her very own. Jane's victory had felt like her own.

While Wade had all the great attributes, Josh had, well, he was just ordinary. He looked like any other farmer in town. He didn't have Wade's six pack of abs. But, he didn't have a beer belly either. He had a broader chest than Wade. Josh's voice was gravely as he talked and joked just a little louder than everyone else. He looked like he had forgotten to shave today, with an obvious layer of stubble on his upper lip and a patch below his lower lip.

Next was the youngest Tucker son, Pete, sitting with his new wife, Mackenzie. Pete had graduated a year ahead of Jane from high school. Jane had told Kiley that Pete and Mackenzie were just staying here until they could save up enough money for their own house. Pete had a wiry frame with dirty blond hair that he kept a little long and shaggy. He appeared to be the quietest of all the boys. Kiley would later find out that Mackenzie had been an only child of a widowed mother. So all the hustle and bustle in this house was very different from how she had grown up. But she appeared to be adjusting just fine.

After dinner, they all sat around talking in the living room, except for Jane and Kiley, who kept nodding off. Jane got up and beckoned to Kiley. She followed Jane upstairs and down the hall. There were four bedrooms upstairs and one bathroom right at the top of the stairs. Another two bedrooms were downstairs, with another one and half bathrooms. Pete and Mackenzie slept downstairs, next to the master bedroom of Evan and Donna.

Jane showed Kiley where her bedroom would be for the duration of her stay. It was the farthest from the stairs and the bathroom. As it was the last of the six bedrooms in the house available, it was also the smallest.

"It is even smaller than the baby's nursery," Jane told her.

The room was narrow. A twin bed was pushed up against the right wall, a dresser and tiny table against the left. There was just enough room to walk through between them. Kiley wondered if the table had been put there just for her, to function as a small desk. A small window with a homemade curtain was over the head of the bed, a tiny closet was at the foot.

"That's OK. Thanks for inviting me to come stay," Kiley said.

"You won't be thanking me when there is a screaming baby keeping you up all night," Jane said, dryly.

"You know, there are plenty of people in this house. You don't really need me around to help," Kiley stated the obvious.

Jane was quiet for a moment, thinking of how to word her response.

"I think I need you here in the house more for my mental well-being than the baby's physical care," Jane explained.

"Oh. Well, then, thank you. I guess."

"Plus, you needed somewhere to crash while you work on your next book, right?" Jane prodded.

"That's true."

"You could have stayed with mom or dad. Or Miley, I guess. But maybe being in your old hometown will spark some inspiration," Jane mused.

"Maybe," Kiley replied, doubtful.

"Just, please, do NOT put a wicked sister in this story."

"Oh, no problem. I have learned my lesson there."

"Goodnight," said Jane.

"Goodnight," echoed Kiley.

Kiley really did want to unpack and sort her things. But after putting on her pajamas and brushing her teeth, she quickly fell asleep on the twin bed with the warm, handmade quilt covering her.

4

Kiley could hear the wooden floors in the hallway of the old farm house protesting as members of the household marched to and from the bathroom. It must be morning, if you could call it that. There was still darkness behind the curtains on her small window. Kiley rolled over, pulling the quilt up high over her ears. She was simply too tired to get up with everyone else. She easily slipped back under the veil of sleep.

A few hours later, there was a knock at the door. Before Kiley could find her voice, Jane peeked in. When she saw Kiley was awake, she opened the door wider, producing a tray of delicious-looking breakfast food.

"Good morning, sleepyhead. I told Donna that your favorite breakfast food was egg muffin sandwiches. As there are no MacRonnell's within 40 miles of us, Donna made you her own version."

"It smells and looks great," Kiley said, her voice still rough from her long night's sleep.

"I hope all the early birds didn't wake you."

"No. I just didn't realize that farmers got up before the sun came up. That is not how it is portrayed in coffee commercials."

"They have plenty to keep them busy, even at such an early hour," Jane explained. Then she thought for a moment, and changed the subject. "I was thinking maybe you would want to go up to Huntington with me this afternoon to do some last minute Christmas shopping."

"But Christmas is still two weeks away," Kiley pointed out.

"Yes, but this will probably be my last chance to shop." Jane pointed to her burgeoning belly.

"Oh, right. Sure, that sounds fun."

"OK. Eat, shower, get dressed. I'll see you downstairs."

"OK."

Kiley had wanted to spend some time unpacking this morning, but decided to skip it. She didn't want to keep Jane waiting. Lord knows, she had been waiting for nine months already.

But as Kiley tried to find her toiletries, a clean T-shirt, and a pair of jeans for today, she realized she would have to revise her plan. She gave up on saving time and took a half an hour to sort her things. When she was finished, there was a giant pile of laundry in the corner of the room by the door. Kiley could not believe all those clothes had fit into her luggage. She would have to tackle that mountain this evening, or live in fear of dying in a laundry avalanche as she slept. She found the towels someone was nice enough to leave on top of the dresser for her; most likely Donna.

Jane had to sit and rest often, but she was on track to make it around the entire mall. Kiley did not seem to be the only one impressed by this. Other shoppers were gawking at how pregnant she seemed to be, and out shopping for fun. Jane said all the walking might help the baby to come sooner. While it was a weekday, and a workday for Wade, he had still come along. He obviously had come in case of emergency, i.e. baby arrival. He was being a mother hen, but he gave Jane and Kiley their privacy to talk and power shop, though not before making sure Jane and Kiley both had their cell phones with them and powered up.

"This is so nice, just having some sister time, isn't it?" Jane asked.

"Yes, it is nice. I can't remember the last time we hung out like this."

"Next time, I will have to push a stroller and schedule diaper changing pit stops."

"You are so overly organized. It is a sickness. The disorganization of having a baby might just drive you nuts," Kiley said, smiling.

"And that is why you are here. To keep me sane."

"Oh, now the evil plot unfolds!" They both laughed.

Kiley stopped suddenly in front of a store window. "Oh. That would be great for my next book tour." It was one of those fashionable ensembles that were intended to be transformable from a day at the office to a night on the town. It had an edge to it, mostly due to the black leather jacket with lots of zippers that went over the more formal top. The black denim pants were slim cut. They would accentuate Kiley's thin figure quite nicely.

"You should try it on," Jane urged.

"Oh, I don't have the funds for something like that. Most of the advance from my first book went to purchase the dress clothes I have worn for the last six months and the car I have been putting miles on."

"Sounds like it is time to get a second book out. How is that coming?" Jane inquired.

"Just notes, so far. I was hoping to get a start on it while I was staying with you."

"Meaning, you have nowhere else to stay rent-free until you get another big paycheck."

"No comment," Kiley replied.

"Excuse me, I couldn't help but overhear. You are K. Riley, aren't you? The author." A middle-aged woman with a friendly face touched Kiley on the elbow.

"Oh, ya, hi. And you are?" Kiley responded. Luckily she was had not forgotten how to put her friendly author face on for the public.

"Betsy. I read your book. I loved it. Well, my daughter read it and passed it on to me. Is it true you are from the area?"

"Yes. I grew up right down the road in Oakley."

"Oh, well, I can't wait for your next book. It is always great to meet a local celebrity," the woman gushed.

"It is so nice to meet a reader. I'm sorry, but I've got to get back to my sister now," Kiley apologized.

"Oh, of course." The woman's voice quickly lost its friendliness. She gave a cold stare toward Jane, before she turned to walk away from them.

"Again with the evil sister. Ugh," Jane groaned and rolled her eyes.

"Try not to take it personally."

"I love how she admitted she was too cheap to buy her own copy of your book. Right to your face!" Jane said, throwing her hands up in the air.

"It isn't about the number of sales, it is about the number of readers. The more exposure I get out of this book might mean more sales for the next one."

Jane's phone rang. She pulled it out of her pocket, sighed, and pushed the talk button.

"No baby. I have your number. I will call you if anything develops," she paused. "OK, bye."

"Wade?" Kiley guessed.

"Of course. He says he got us a table at Smokin' Eddie's. We should head out there. I can't wait to get a big ol' BBQ pork sandwich."

"You are hungry again? We just ate lunch a few hours ago."

"Ya, and I've had a lot of exercise since then."

Wade, Jane, and Kiley had a nice sit-down dinner. It would probably be the last dinner out Wade and Jane would have before becoming parents. They were at the restaurant so long that Jane excused herself to call Donna, so that she would not worry about them. The mall had closed by the time they had finished. Being chivalrous, Wade walked around the outside of the mall to retrieve the car they had parked in the furthest parking lot. He came back and picked up Jane and Kiley at the door. Jane climbed into the back seat so she could put up her swollen ankles. She soon nodded off. Wade spent the rest of the trip filling Kiley in on all the local Oakley news and gossip. She asked him about her former classmates, most of whom were too young for Wade to know.

It was late when they got back to the farmhouse. Kiley got a sinking feeling as she remembered Mt. Saint Dirty Sock in her bedroom. It was too late tonight to do multiple loads of laundry. That chore would have to wait till tomorrow.

"Oh, there you are. I was just about to call," Donna declared, her voice filled with concern.

"I can't believe you are still up," Kiley said.

"Oh, I'm always up this time of night. I actually got off early from the bar tonight. Otherwise I would have been there till 1:00AM. At least they take pity on me and don't make me close anymore."

"Good to know. If I need something baked at midnight, I'll look you up," Kiley joked.

"Oh, honey, I washed up all those clothes for you. I assumed a large pile in the corner equaled dirty."

"Thanks, but you didn't have to do that," Kiley said, surprised.

"Don't worry," Donna continued. "I noticed that some of them were dress clothes and I followed the tag instructions for them. You will have to do it yourself next time. I was just helping out."

"Thanks. I don't even pay attention to that."

Kiley went on up to her bedroom. She found neat stacks of folded clothes on her bed. She buried her nose into a pile, as if to prove to herself they were actually clean. An artificial fresh scent filled her nose. You sure didn't get this type of service at a hotel, even if it was a one-time introductory offer. She pulled open the drawers on the dresser and used the "Eeny, meeny, miny, moe" method of deciding which drawer things would go into. It would make it interesting in the morning to discover where she had put everything. It could be like a treasure hunt.

5

Kiley woke up late again the next morning. The only person who seemed to be home besides herself was Jane. She found Jane watching TV in the living room. Apparently Jane had tried to go to work in the farm office, where she had run things for the past several years. But they had all thrown her out and sent her back home. With Kiley here now, Jane wouldn't be alone in the house. She suspected that the men didn't want to be first responders if Jane started to have contractions. They probably had not even begun to think about the mess they would have on their hands if her water broke in the office.

Kiley grabbed an apple for breakfast out of the ever-present fruit bowl in the pass-through window to the kitchen. It was one of those small apples they sold at the grocery store in big bags. The other kids at elementary school usually had them in their lunches packed with love from home. Miley and Kiley always had school lunches, because their mother did not have time to pack lunches before work. Kiley had always been envious of the other kids and their small apples.

She plunked down on the couch across from Jane, her laptop bag swinging onto the cushion next to her. She hadn't checked her email in two days. Being in Oakley was like being sucked into a time warp. Kiley could lose herself here if she was not careful. She had to unplug a lamp in order to plug in her laptop with the dead battery.

One of her many unanswered emails was from her publisher. Their fiscal year was ending on December 31st, and she needed to turn in any reimbursement forms (with the supporting receipts) before then. Kiley sighed and unzipped the front pocket of her laptop bag, where she had been stuffing three months' worth of receipts. They fell all around her like snow in Alaska. Jane raised an eyebrow at her sister.

"Isn't the life of a published author glamorous?"

"Yes, that is exactly what I was thinking," Jane replied.

"I will probably be doing this all day," Kiley sighed.

"Wouldn't your time be better spent writing?"

"One would think. But this is where the real money is made: travel reimbursements," Kiley said, smiling.

They were quiet for a while. The only sounds were the commercials on TV, promising new and improved, and Kiley crinkling receipts. Dave the dog, having become accustomed to Kiley's presence, lay snoring in the corner.

"So you really don't know the sex of the baby?" Kiley's voice broke into the background sounds.

"I told you that when you asked me what to buy for it. Neutral colors."

Kiley had been traveling when Jane had her baby shower, but had shipped her gifts along to Oakley.

"But I thought maybe you and Wade knew, and just weren't telling anyone else."

"Nope. Trust me, it would be so much easier to buy things like car seats and curtains if I knew. All the cute baby stuff is geared toward either boys or girls. I guess Wade and I are just old-fashioned that way."

"You still have time to find out," Kiley prodded.

"Seriously. I waited this long. I think I can wait two more weeks. Plus, it feels like a boy."

"A boy? That is just what this house needs, another male. And how do you know?" Kiley inquired.

"I don't. It is just a feeling I have," Jane responded.

"Ugh. I don't think I ever want to have any kids."

"Maybe you should find someone you love first, then decide."

"That is a much nicer answer than the one mom gave me," Kiley griped.

"That's because she is already a mom. I'm not—yet." They both laughed.

"I thought you and Wade bought a house. Why are you still living here?"

"Oh, didn't I tell you?" Jane paused while she grimaced and put a throw pillow behind her back. "We bought it last summer and it was a fixer-upper. We figured in a few months we could be moved in. But every time we tried to make a cosmetic fix, it led to something larger. Remove the old floor to put down hardwood—find old termite damage. Put in a new toilet and vanity in the bathroom—discover all new pipes are needed. Plan to re-shingle the roof and discover it needs to have all the main boards replaced. Have you ever heard the term 'money pit'?"

"No."

"Well, that is our house. So, we are paying a mortgage and repair costs at the same time, and we don't even get to live there. We can't move in now until it has heat and the mold is gone. Don't want to move a newborn into a cold, moldy house."

"Well, you should take me there sometime, so I can see it. I hope it has a guest bedroom for me."

"Sure, but it has two twin beds. You will have to share with Miley."

"Oh, it will be like old times."

As the day wore on, Evan and Wade came home for lunch, and to check on Jane as well. Donna came home from her morning shift at the Diner and went upstairs to take a nap before her evening shift at the bar. Kiley could not understand how someone could enjoy working so much, especially when she didn't have to. Evan would be more than able to care for anything Donna might need.

Kiley could not stand the thought of possibly having to get a real job to pay rent regularly. She had an English degree. That really only set her up to be a teacher or work at a publishing company. Maybe a newspaper. Oh wait, those were dinosaurs now, quickly becoming extinct. Writing books was work too, but at least she could set her own hours. Sometimes writer's block had other ideas.

That evening, everyone began streaming in the door after their long day. Donna made dinner for everyone, then headed out halfway through the meal to make the start of her shift at the bar. Kiley was going to have to take her aside one of these days and have a discussion with her about being underappreciated. Everyone seemed to show up for dinner except for Josh. The usual chatter accompanied the meal. Kiley found out that Mackenzie had the job that Jane and Kiley's mom once held as a file clerk. She found out that Jane had a doctor's appointment tomorrow. She made plans to go with her.

After dinner, everyone did their own thing. Kiley spent some time by herself in her room. She tried to read a book, but it couldn't hold her attention. After she heard what seemed like a million feet in the hallway heading to bed, she grabbed her laptop and headed back downstairs. She turned on *Third Shift with Timmy Killon* on TV, careful to keep the volume low, and curled up on the couch to do some mindless Internet surfing. The dog jumped up on the couch and curled up next to her.

Dave was an orange mutt. His tan eyes looked like they were outlined with thick black eyeliner. From the tennis ball catching skills Kiley had witnessed outside, Dave was most likely a retriever mix. He was a really beautiful dog. Kiley mindlessly scratched his ears.

About a half hour later, Kiley was startled by the sound of the front door. Dave didn't move until Josh's broad-shouldered body came into view. She put her front paws on the floor, leaving her back paws on the couch, and proceeded to give a big stretch before approaching Josh. She gave him the royal sniff down.

"Well, hey there," Josh smiled a wide grin at Kiley. All his teeth showed. It reminded her of the Cheshire cat.

"Hey," she replied, guarded.

"I haven't seen you since you arrived. I thought maybe we scared you off."

"Nope. I have to stay to meet my new niece or nephew."

"You are going to make a great aunt...or uncle."

Kiley looked at him to see if he was serious, but he was already rooting around with his head in the refrigerator.

"Any leftovers?"

"No. I am hoarding them all in my room," Kiley said, trying to play along.

"Didn't think there was room for a mini fridge in there." Josh started to eat a leftover pork chop. No fork, no knife, no plate; only his hand and mouth.

"There isn't."

"That room is gonna stink in a few weeks."

"Maybe Dave will help me finish it," Kiley said. Dave's triangular ear twitched with the sound of his name.

"Oh, now don't you go feeding my dog human food. That's a bad habit."

"He is your dog?"

"Yes, SHE is."

"Dave is a girl?" Kiley asked, surprised.

"Don't act so surprised," Josh replied.

"How did that happen?"

"She showed up as a puppy at the back door. I asked what her name was. She told me Dave. It is not a difficult story to follow."

"Maybe a little difficult to believe."

"You don't believe she told me?" Josh cocked up one eyebrow before he continued. "You just hang around her for a while, you'll see."

Kiley looked at Dave. Dave stood at the foot of the stairs, glancing up, then back to Josh.

"See? She just told me it was time for bed. See you at breakfast. Oh wait, I forgot. You can't get up that early."

Before Kiley could think of a good retort, he was up the stairs and out of sight. Talking to him had been an exercise in frustration. Any energy she had left was now drained away. She turned off the TV and her computer, and headed upstairs. She noticed that there was a glow coming from under the door of the bedroom next to hers. That must be his room, she thought. There was a biohazard sticker on the door.

He was one to talk. His room had already been labeled as dangerous.

6

The next week went by very fast. Kiley went with Jane to her doctor's appointment. An ultrasound showed that the baby was breech. Kiley tried to look for a penis on the ultrasound, but could only make out the giant alien skull. She hoped in a week the baby's body would grow to be more in proportion with its head. The doctor scheduled a cesarean for the following Wednesday. Everyone in the Tucker household seemed very twitterpated about this. Jane still tried to stay active to coax the baby out sooner, although that would require a rush to the hospital because it would still have to come out by surgery. Hopefully it wouldn't prove terribly inconvenient that the closest full-service hospital was two-and-a-half hours away.

Preparations for Christmas were started now, so that not as much would have to be done after the baby came. Two giant fresh turkeys suddenly appeared at the Tucker household. Luckily they had a second refrigerator in the garage to hold them. One large and one small Christmas tree were brought into the house. Kiley helped decorate them. She loved the smell of a live Christmas tree. It really made it feel like Christmas was near. Donna loved live trees too. That is why she always got them, even though she was allergic. She would double-up on her allergy medication to counteract the symptoms. This also seemed to have the side effect of making her extra jolly.

Wade seemed to be a wreck up until the day before the surgery. Then he seemed to reach some sort of Zen. Jane, on the other hand, was fine up until the night before, then she was having a major freak-out. While Jane insisted that she had actually wanted to have a C-section all along, she was still nervous about being awake while being cut open. Jane only slept two hours that night. Most of that time, Kiley was sitting up with her, trying to distract her from thinking about the upcoming surgery she would undergo.

While Jane was asleep, Kiley headed out in the middle of the night to the 24-hour gas station, Qwik Serv, to stock up on hospital snacks and coke. She knew she would need some, but bought enough for everyone else as well. They had a small rack with copies of her book on the checkout counter. Must be her agent's doing. She pulled out a pen and quickly autographed all the copies before returning them to the display. The cashier raised an eyebrow, but said nothing. Neither he nor Kiley knew each other. She could have been drawing dirty pictures in them for all he knew. When she got back to the farmhouse, she met Josh in the kitchen.

"Wow, you are up early enough for breakfast...for once," he added. He took a carton of eggs out of the fridge, and walked over to a waiting frying pan on the stove.

"I haven't been to bed yet." A yawn slipped out as if to prove Kiley's point. She sat down on a bar stool in the living room, looking across the pass-through into the kitchen.

"Did you find someone to hook up with? Slim pickin' in this town."

"If I had known you were the one cooking breakfast, maybe I would get up early more often. You know, just to see if you can actually cook," Kiley said, ignoring his previous question.

"Oh, ya. I can cook. I am red hot." He winked at Kiley.

"Mmm-hmm," was all Kiley gave him in return.

"You should try some of what I'm offering, J.K."

"What did you call me?"

"J.K."

"For your information, I write under just the initial 'K.' "

"J.K. Ya know, like that chick who writes the books about the boy wizard."

"What about her?"

"You're an author, she's an author. I think I'll just call you J.K."

"OK, I am way too tired to be having this conversation with you," she replied. Kiley waved her hands in front of her, as if trying to clear away his nonsense.

"Not O-K. J-K. Geez...," he shook his head as a smile played across his lips. Kiley could sense that he found this joke funny and wasn't about to let it go anytime soon.

Jane appeared in the kitchen.

"You want something? I'll make you whatever you want," Josh offered helpfully, using his spatula to point into the already hot frying pan where the eggs were gently popping on top of a bed of butter.

"No, I am not supposed to eat this morning." Turning to Kiley, Jane continued, "Wade and I were going to get an early start to the hospital. We are going to head out in a few minutes... Unless, of course, you want to eat first." Jane gave her a pleading look.

"No, I'm good. Got snacks." Kiley shook her white plastic bag for emphasis, then hopped off of the stool to follow Jane upstairs. Jane might need her help to carry a bag or something.

"Missing breakfast again, Miss Rowling? I see a habit forming. Don't you know that breakfast is the most important meal of the day?"

Josh kept rambling on, but his voice faded as she climbed the stairs.

"Doesn't he ever shut up?" Kiley asked. Jane was close enough to hear her, but lost in her own world. It was mostly a rhetorical question, anyway.

Kiley fell asleep in the backseat of the vehicle almost immediately after they pulled out of the driveway. She didn't have the full backseat to stretch out, because the child seat had already been placed in Jane's car to transport the baby home. Hopefully Wade could take a shift at distracting Jane's thoughts.

7

The hospital was a lot of waiting. Kiley was glad she had brought her notebook to write in. Except she was tired and distracted, and filled the pages with only doodles. Evan, Donna, and Mackenzie showed up just after Jane and Wade went back into the delivery room. In less than an hour, Wade emerged carrying a blanket in his arms. The newborn was so tiny you would never know it was wrapped in the blanket if this wasn't the maternity ward. Jane came along behind, being pushed along on a gurney and unconscious. Her appearance was actually pretty frightening.

In the room, Jane came to in about ten minutes. No one noticed except for Kiley and the nurse. Everyone else was fussing over the baby. Kiley felt a little sorry for Jane. Especially since she was throwing up as she came out of the anesthesia. She had grown this being inside her for nine months and experienced God knows what in the delivery room. Now everyone else got to see the new baby before she did. It didn't seem fair.

Within an hour, Jane was still loopy, but well enough to hold her little boy. At 5 pounds, 11 ounces, he was just a tiny thing. Evan had said all his boys had come out 8 pounds or more. Jane said she felt sorry for his wife. Everyone agreed that maybe Jane would just have small babies. She told them she wasn't having any more. Everyone was on a baby high except her, and said she would change her mind. They named him Ethan Riley Tucker. Wade and Jane arranged it so that he would have the same initials as Wade's father, Evan. He said this would cause confusion when they initialed the invoices in the office. He pretended to be annoyed by this. He would have to make sure to retire by the time Ethan started working there. He tried to hide the joy in his voice.

At first, Kiley tried to hang back in case Jane needed anything. But Jane was pretty out of it and wanted to sleep. Then Kiley followed the Tuckers around. This included stops in the cafeteria and the gift shop. Wade was to stay the night at the hospital with Jane. Kiley left a large supply of her snacks behind with Wade (he was very appreciative), then rode home with the Tuckers.

Dave greeted them when they got home, sniffing all the strange hospital smells they had brought back with them. Mackenzie gave Pete a kiss, then insisted she needed a shower to get the hospital germs off of her. Kiley saw no sign of Josh. Kiley headed upstairs to her bedroom, and Dave followed.

"You want to stay in here, puppy?" she asked, before closing the door to the hallway. Dave hesitantly came in and sniffed around, apparently unsure if she would be welcome. Kiley was so tired she changed her clothes and went right to bed.

Kiley woke up to a knock on her bedroom door around 1:00AM. Josh poked his head in, turning on the light.

"What is it? Is it Jane?" Kiley asked, extremely groggy but alarmed.

"No. You stole my dog."

Dave now lay curled up on the bed next to Kiley. Actually, Dave was hogging the bed. Dave raised her head and greeted Josh with a wag of her bushy orange tail, but gave no indication she was going to leave the cushy spot she had found.

Josh snapped the light off and shut the door, muttering, "Whatever. Traitor," under his breath.

8

The good part about sleeping with Dave was that she kept the bed warm. She also afforded a degree of security in an unfamiliar house. The bad part about sleeping with Dave was that she was accustomed to being let outside early in the morning to do her business. She started fussing and pacing. When she threw in a whimper, Kiley had to get up. She threw on her white, terry cloth robe that she may have accidentally packed in her luggage at some long-forgotten hotel, and followed Dave down the stairs to let her out. As Kiley waited for her to finish her business, she wandered into the kitchen. She ran into Josh.

"Ah, so that is how to get you up early in the morning, J.K. Shut a dog in your room."

"She was a good bedmate."

"I bet there are better ones in this house."

Kiley ignored him and went to let Dave back in again. When she came back, Evan had entered the kitchen as well.

"Oh, Kiley. Donna wanted me to tell you that we are going to head up to the hospital right after she gets off at the Diner at 1:00PM. Apparently the baby started to show signs of jaundice in the night, so they had to put him under a light in the nursery. Fairly common. Nothing to be too concerned about," Evan explained.

"Oh, OK. I'll be ready."

"Ah, so you will be joining us for breakfast today, I presume?" Josh tried to impersonate a French chef, but his gravelly voice threw it off.

"Guess so."

Kiley knew Josh couldn't throw any more suggestive comments at her as his family quickly began to fill up the kitchen table.

Kiley was surprised when she walked into the hospital room to see her twin sister Miley and her mother sitting by Jane's bed. She hugged them both and told them how much she had missed them, slightly more emphatically for her sister. Her mom looked the same as always, thin with her brown hair just a little messy. Their mom wore her glasses all the time now, not just when she was reading or typing like she used to when Kiley was young. It was hard for Kiley to get used to. Her mother had a few more wrinkles around her eyes, and looked a bit tired.

The baby happened to be in the room right then, instead of the nursery. This was because Miley and her mom had wanted to hold him. The baby still had a light under his blanket. A cord came out and plugged into the wall. The light was eerie and made the baby look like a human glow worm. Jane made Kiley take a picture of it, for future inclusion in Ethan's baby book.

Kiley and Miley were starting to catch one another up on what was happening in their lives. They were actually planning on heading to the cafeteria, when the nurse spoke to Jane.

"Riley is a nice name," she commented on the baby's middle name, written on the ID card in the hospital-issued bassinette.

"It is my maiden name," Jane replied.

"I am reading a book by some guy named Riley now. K. Riley."

"Is that *Don't Judge A Boy By His Shoes?*" Jane inquired.

"Why, yes it is. Have you read it?" the nurse asked.

"Yes. My sister Kiley over there wrote it," Jane gestured to Kiley.

"Oh, wow! That is so cool. If I go get my copy, will you autograph it?" the nurse asked, turning to Kiley.

"Sure, of course," she replied.

The nurse fled the room.

"How much do you want to bet she will forget to bring my pain meds back with her?" Jane half-joked.

"Wow, little sister. You are all famous now and junk," Miley teased.

"I have been trying to tell you guys that for a year now," Kiley said sarcastically.

"And we are all so proud of you," her mother said, like a robot who was programmed to.

The nurse burst back into the room, carrying the book and a pen, but very obviously no pills.

"Oh, this is so cool. Make it out to Erin. That's E-R-I-N."

"I am glad you are enjoying it," Kiley said, as she took the book and pen from her, turning to a blank page near the front.

"My friend and I agree this story does for *Cinderella* what *10 Things I Hate About You* did for *The Taming of The Shrew*."

"Well, thanks." Kiley always accepted new theories about her book.

"Thank you. Will your next book be a sequel?"

"Oh, no, I think sequels are for lazy writers. They don't want to have to come up with a new set of original characters again," Kiley replied.

"Oh, that's sad. I had kind of grown attached to them."

"Make sure you take good care of my sister, alright?" Kiley handed her back the now autographed book as a kind of bribe. She didn't want Jane to get poor care because Kiley had written an evil sister in her book.

9

After the nurse left the room, Kiley headed with Miley down to the hospital cafeteria, so that they could talk beyond the prying ears of their mother. Most people who met them as adults never realized that Miley and Kiley were identical twins, Miley being the older of the two. It was amazing what a few bottles of hair color could do. Kiley had kept her hair in a bob with bangs and dyed black since she was sixteen years old. Her sister, on the other hand, always wore her hair long and highlighted blond. In the last few years, there were more highlights than lowlights. While they didn't often agree on anything, they still counted each other as best friends. Kiley counted herself grateful to have such a close relationship with her sister, even if Miley often displayed very shallow behavior.

"Are you so happy to be off the road?" Miley asked.

"I am. All that traveling was fun, but now I need a break," Kiley replied.

They went through the cafeteria line. Kiley got a can of Coca-Cola and a chicken breast with mashed potatoes. After all the convenience store junk yesterday, she needed to make amends with her stomach today and eat something at least slightly resembling real food. Miley got a bottle of water and a salad. Kiley wasn't sure if she was dieting or being thrifty, or both.

"So, you are still in the same apartment here in Huntington, right?"

"Yes. Moving out of the house where Mom and Aunt Jamie are and getting my own place was the best decision I ever made. Mom kept nagging me to 'do something' with my life. With my own place, I can do what I want, be lazy when I want, invite over who I want."

"So, the party planning business must be going well if you can afford your own place all by yourself."

"Well…mostly."

"Mile, what's the real story?"

"I needed a little help making rent. And Sandy and I are getting along really well right now…"

"Sandy? Ick, Mile. You can do better than that smarmy playboy." Kiley had met Sandy once, and he didn't leave a good impression. He had black hair that he wore slicked back, and usually with a black goatee and moustache. With his thick eyebrows, it just made him look like a villain out of a cartoon.

"Don't talk that way about the man I love."

"How long, exactly, has he been living with you?"

"Since the second month after I got the apartment."

"Miley! That has been like six months now. And how many times have you two broke up in that time?"

"I wouldn't call it broken up. Separated, maybe."

"Was Sandy dating other women during this time?"

"There were one or two, a few," Miley admitted.

"But you two were still sharing the apartment during that time?"

"Yes. But there are two bedrooms. Depending on where we are in our relationship, sometimes we are sleeping in the same bedroom, and sometimes we are not."

"And Mom is alright with you living with Sandy?"

"Of course," Miley responded.

"Really? Cuz I can go up to the room and ask her."

"Of course...she thinks that Sandy is a woman."

"Miley."

"I didn't lie to her. Mom just assumed, and I never corrected her. Don't tell her. She would FREAK if she knew."

"Mom would get used to the idea. Jane and Wade lived together before they were married."

"It was different with Jane. She was the oldest and was always allowed to do whatever she wanted."

Kiley ranked this as a false statement in her own mind. Jane had never broken any rules growing up. No drinking, no drugs—Jane had never so much as smoked a cigarette. Wade was the one exception to Jane's freakishly stellar behavior.

"So, that sounds like a hot mess waiting to happen. How is the business?" Miley was now co-owner of the party planning business Jenny Jones had started years ago. Jenny was better known for being the town librarian.

"It is going better than it ever has. With me living in Huntington, I am poised to book us better events than Jenny could from Oakley. I can put in full-time effort, because I don't have another job like she does. I also have a better sense of marketing, if I do say so myself. Saturday a huge holiday party is planned at the Country Club, for all its loyal members. It is a really big deal to be hired for the job. I enlisted the best of the best caterers, my best friend Travis. God, I have been doing all the talking. So, tell me all about what it is like to live in the Tucker house?"

"Haven't you asked Jane about this? She has been staying with them longer than I have," Kiley said. She ran her thumbs around the top of the coke can in front of her.

"Yes. But she just gives me boring answers—crowded, noisy, good food."

"All those things are true," Kiley agreed.

"Kiley!"

"Well, they are."

"I expect more out of you. You are my twin. We think alike," Miley said.

"We haven't thought alike since we hit puberty," Kiley deadpanned.

"Does Randy still look like a younger version of his dad?"

"Um, he doesn't live at home anymore."

"Why are Pete and his wife still living there?"

"I don't know."

"C'mon. Do Donna and Evan fight? Is there any dirt? Does Wade walk around the house shirtless?"

"C'mon, no. They are a nice, normal, loving family. Donna and Evan get along great. The only one that's strange seems to be Josh...," Kiley said.

"Josh! Wait, which one is he again?"

"He is the one that looks like he could start a motorcycle gang."

"Oh. He was always the most mischievous. I think he got arrested once."

Kiley made a mental note to grill Josh on that interesting tidbit at a later time.

"He is always the last one to come home at night. And somehow I always run into him downstairs. I don't know how he can stay out at the bar so late drinking and still be the first one up in the morning," Kiley wondered.

"Ooo. Sounds like you have a crush on him... He is the only single guy in that house. Well, besides your new nephew."

"Ack, no! He is like, an asshole." Kiley thought for a moment. "He does have a great dog, though."

"Josh and Kiley, sittin' in a tree—"

"Miley, hon', you ready to head out?" their mother interrupted them. Kiley checked her cell. The sisters had been talking for two hours before their mom came down to the cafeteria to find them.

"Oh, sure. How are Jane and the baby doing?" Miley asked.

"OK. They still want to keep the baby under the light at least until tomorrow. I hope they make it home by Christmas," their mom fretted.

"Bye, guys. Good luck with your party, Miley. Merry Christmas, Mom," Kiley called. She would most likely not see her again until after Christmas. Kiley did not get up from her spot at the table, and continued to run her thumbs around the top of her coke can.

"You have a nice holiday too, honey," her mother said, and paused. Miley walked on out the cafeteria door. "I'm glad you are back here near family."

"Oh. Thanks, Mom. It's nice to sleep in the same bed every night," Kiley replied.

Their mom smiled, then looked down, shook her head, and left the room.

It seemed like Kiley's answer did not satisfy her mother. In what way it was lacking, Kiley had no clue. She couldn't bring herself to be warm and gooey with her mother. She had never seen any indication that her mother even had that in her, and had therefore never instilled it into her daughters.

Kiley finally pulled herself up and headed for the elevators, back to Jane's room. It was amazing how much a hospital could drain you, just suck all the life right out of you. The harshness of the fluorescent lights made her eyes tired. The cushioned chairs were all uncomfortable. The illusion of cleanliness was broken anytime you looked too closely at what didn't get picked up off the floors. The nurses were there when you didn't want them, and absent when you did. The patient having to eat and take medication and go to the bathroom and give blood on the hospital's schedule; they have their normal bodily functions taken out of their own control. Kiley didn't understand how anyone could actually get better in this environment.

10

Wade and Jane and baby Ethan stayed in the hospital for two more days. Kiley went on the third day of their stay, Friday, because she thought they would be released then. But they were kept until Saturday, Christmas Eve. Kiley stayed home that day. Donna assured her that she and Evan could handle getting the baby, the proud parents, and any gifts and flowers home without her. Instead, Kiley tried to clean anything she could think of before the baby arrived home.

It turned out that the offices of Tucker Farms were shut down altogether the week before and after Christmas. The guys still went out to do the daily chores, but nothing that could wait. That meant there were a lot of other people underfoot as Kiley tried to vacuum, do dishes, laundry, etc. Her efforts seemed to begrudgingly inspire the others as well. Soon Pete and Mackenzie started to half-heartedly help. Josh, well, he gave Dave a bath. That seemed to be the extent of his ability to do chores on Christmas Eve.

When the car arrived home from the hospital, everyone filled the living room to gush over the baby. They all took turns holding him. There was a fire crackling in the fireplace. The Christmas tree lights shone brightly. The presents overflowed from under the tree. Most of the gifts were for the new arrival, no doubt.

It was all so beautiful and perfect that it made bile rise in Kiley's throat. It was like eating a chocolate frosted chocolate chip brownie; too sweet. She wasn't sure why, but she had to get out of that room. She quietly excused herself, saying she was tired. Donna stopped her at the base of the stairs, thanking her for all the housework she had done, and it was no wonder she was so tired. Dave followed Kiley upstairs to her bedroom, as was the new custom. They both laid on the small bed. Kiley fell asleep stroking the soft velvet of Dave's ears.

Kiley woke up to a knock on her bedroom door.

"Kiley, honey, Merry Christmas. We are going to open gifts soon. Are you awake in there?" Donna said through the door.

"Yes. Be right down," Kiley croaked.

She looked around for her terry cloth robe, but couldn't find it. She found a long flannel shirt that could pass as a robe. She threw it on over her stretched out T-shirt and pajama pants.

She brushed her hair and brushed her teeth, and then headed downstairs.

It was a madhouse! Breakfast seemed to be hot chocolate and Christmas cookies. Kiley poured herself a mug of hot chocolate. She added mini marshmallows, which quickly melted into a sugary glaze on top. She grabbed five frosted Christmas cookies. The way this family ate, she didn't want to chance coming back for seconds and finding an empty plate.

Jane rested on the couch, feeding the baby a bottle as he lay nestled in her arms. Donna sat between her and Evan. Everyone else was on the floor in their pajamas, grabbing for gifts.

They looked like ten year olds, instead of adults in their twenties and thirties, as they actually were. Wade and Josh were the worst. They grabbed at gifts and shook them, before even reading the gift tags. They were even smelling them.

"Don't open anything until Randy gets here!" Donna protested.

As if on cue, the doorbell rang.

Wade and Josh raced each other to the door, tripping each other on the way. Soon Randy and his wife, Violet, and their two children, Mary and Johnny, had joined the melee. Mary looked to be about five, while Johnny proudly proclaimed to everyone he had recently turned "free." They looked like a family out of an insurance commercial. Randy was the tall, dark, and handsome father. Violet wore her motherly exhaustion on face while flashing everyone a beautiful smile. The kids both had hair the color of maple syrup, a perfect mixture of Randy's black and Violet's blond. Kiley could picture them all on the television inside her head, standing in front of a two-story house, complete with a basketball hoop on the garage, and Mary and Johnny playing soccer with each other before lining up with mom and dad for the logo and jingle.

Violet couldn't wait to hold the new baby. The other kids seemed to understand the obvious: they would soon have competition for attention at family gatherings. Kiley pictured that as the same look—times two—that Jane must have had at age three when her parents brought home TWO babies.

Everyone started opening gifts. As Kiley had suspected, most of the gifts were for Ethan. To Wade's delight and Josh's chagrin, Wade got to open all of the baby's gifts as Jane had the sleeping bundle of joy in her lap. Kiley had trouble keeping track of who got what. Gifts kept coming Kiley's way. She received more gifts than she had given. She had only bought gifts for Jane, Wade, the baby, and Donna and Evan. She hardly knew anyone else, but they had all managed to get her something—mostly gift cards, as they were the perfect gift for someone you didn't actually know.

A big box came toward Kiley. The tag said, "To: Kiley, From: Jane." Kiley shot her sister a questioning glance, and tore off the wrapping paper. There was never an opportunity for Jane to buy her anything, unless she had purchased it before

Kiley arrived. She pried open the cardboard box to find the dress clothes she had seen in the window at the mall—the day-to-night ensemble. The black leather jacket with all the zippers was even in there.

"You shouldn't have." Kiley tried to admonish Jane, but couldn't hide her giant smile.

"I wanted to show you how proud I was of you. I hope it fits. I had Donna check the sizes on your laundry for me," Jane said.

"That's why you did my laundry that first day!" Kiley turned to accuse Donna, who was just heading to the kitchen to hide. Or to get more cookies. Most likely both.

"Here. I got you a great gift, too." Kiley was surprised by Josh handing her another large box.

"You shouldn't have," Kiley said, confused.

"You already told your sister that. C'mon. Open it," Josh urged.

Kiley hesitated. She hoped it wasn't filled with snakes or something. She opened the box and took out what appeared to be a large, colored pillow inside.

"A dog bed?"

"Ha, ha. You Riley girls are smart."

"I don't get it," Kiley complained.

"Well, I figured that twin bed must be getting crowded with you and Dave both sleeping in it. And she needed a new bed anyway, so I figured it could go in your room," he explained.

"So, you got your dog a gift for Christmas and put my name on it?" she summarized.

"No. That's not it at all." Now it was Josh's turn to look confused.

"He always does that," Randy said.

"He always finds a way to give you a gift that isn't really a gift," Wade yelled.

"Well, Dave can't open it herself...," Josh added.

"Then, thanks. I guess."

Kiley called for Dave to come over and check out her new bed. She sniffed it vigorously, tail wagging.

Kiley took her gifts upstairs and changed into her favorite holey jeans and a worn rose-colored sweatshirt, soft from repeated washings. The neck was so stretched out that it slid off her right shoulder, exposing her bra strap of the same color. She met Josh in the hallway as she left her bedroom. His brawny frame blocked her path.

"I hope the bed, uh, the dog bed was an OK gift?" he asked her. His mouth hung open in uncertainty when he finished speaking. It drew Kiley's attention to the stubble on his chin, under his bottom lip.

"Ah, ya. It was great, after you explained it to me. I'm sorry I didn't get you anything," Kiley told him. She shrugged.

"Aw, no worries. You can double-up on gifts for me next Christmas." With that, he turned around and went into his own bedroom.

Kiley just shook her head. Who knew where she would be next Christmas? That realization made her eager to join in the festivities downstairs, while she could.

11

It was late. Like 11:00PM late. Randy and Violet had gone home to go tuck their overstimulated children into their beds for the night. Everyone was asleep in the Tucker farmhouse, except the few goofy souls in the living room, drinking beer to close out Christmas. That would be Wade, Josh, and Kiley. Someone had put in a DVD of National Lampoon's Christmas Vacation. But Wade and Josh argued over which scenes were the best so often that it made it hard to follow the movie, which everyone knew by heart anyway. If Kiley had her way, she would be watching her yule log DVD of a crackling fire. She found it more relaxing then an actual fireplace because she didn't have to be concerned about fire safety. She idly wondered if that was still at her mother's house.

Just then her cell phone rang. She jumped up off the couch and looked at the screen to see who it was. Her mom and dad had already called her earlier, so there was no mystery who the call would be from. She walked into the kitchen before she answered it.

"Hey, Merry Christmas," she cooed into the phone.

"Hey, you stole my line. Sorry to call so late. You know I am out here in L.A. with my family. So we were real busy all day. And there is the time difference," Ted rattled on.

"Oh, sure. Of course. I'm just glad you called. I miss you." 'Dammit!' Kiley admonished herself. She wanted to see if Ted would say it first.

"You, too."

Or at all. Sure, Kiley could have called Ted herself earlier in the day. But this was the first she had heard from him since she had been in Oakley. No emails, no texts. Three weeks with no communication. This had sort of been Kiley's little test. A Christmas phone call meant keep him, no call meant dump him. They were supposed to be boyfriend and girlfriend, even if it wasn't the ideal flowers and candy situation. And long distance relationships were tough on everyone, right?

"So, how's it going there? Did your sister's thing go OK?" he asked, distracted.

"The birth of my nephew? Ya, it was fine. He had jaundice, so they had to put him under a special light for like three days."

"Huh. Cool. Congrats or whatever. Was he crawling all over in the wrapping paper?"

The distance between them was a result of more than just the physical miles.

"No, you dork. He is only like five days old. He doesn't do anything yet, except eat and sleep and poop."

"Only five days? You have been there for three weeks." Ah, so he did know how long he had not called her.

"Ya, it was nice to spend some time with my sister before her life got all filled up with baby. My last chance, you know," Kiley said.

"That's why I haven't called. I figured you would be all girl bonding and stuff."

Dammit to hell! Kiley had provided another excuse for Ted, another doubt in her brain. Maybe that was the only reason he hadn't called. How could she tell? He was the only real boyfriend she had ever had. Just then Josh came into the kitchen to poke around in the refrigerator.

"So, how is Los Angeles?" Kiley asked, as Josh grabbed a bowl of baked beans and a platter of deviled eggs leftover from dinner and went back to the living room. Viewing his food choices and knowing their expected results to his digestive system, Kiley wished her room was further away from his.

"Oh, L.A. is great. Sunny, warm. We took a tour of Paramount Studios a couple days ago. It was awesome. My sister wanted to take the cheesy bus tour that stalks the stars' homes. I totally vetoed that." Kiley was jealous. She would love to take one of those cheesy tours someday. But apparently it would not be with Ted. "Look, uh, I kinda gotta run. I'll tell you all about it later. Hey, can you send some autographed copies of your book out here to my cousins? They would love it. I'll shoot you their addresses in email."

"I don't have a lot of cash on me right now," Kiley tried to weasel her way out of it.

"No problem. I'll pay you back later," he assured her.

"OK." That didn't really solve the problem. Books were expensive to ship.

"Talk to you later. Bye."

"Bye. I lo—" Kiley stopped herself at the same instant the phone line disconnected.

Weren't a couple supposed to say "I love you" to each other? Kiley was kind of furious at the moment. If Ted had been right in front of her in person, she probably would have broken up with him right then. But he wasn't. And it was much nicer to be able to tell people she had a boyfriend. He was in Fredrickstown, Georgia, working on his degree, five hours away. It could be weeks before they would see each other again. And by then, well, all this drama will have blown over.

Kiley calmed herself in the kitchen before returning to the living room with Heckle and Jeckle. She could go upstairs, but she wasn't tired yet and didn't feel like being by herself. She was still fuming over her phone call with Ted. She sat back down on the couch and stared toward the TV, not really seeing the pictures, just the pixels.

"So who was that?" Josh asked, a wide smile spreading across his face. He shoved an entire deviled egg into his mouth and somehow kept smiling.

"My boyfriend," Kiley answered, trying to not give away any hint of her foul mood.

"Oooooo," Wade crowed.

"Wait, there's a boyfriend? How come you never told me you were cheating on me?" Josh bugged his eyes out and let his mouth hang open. Luckily the egg had disappeared.

"There has always been a boyfriend," Kiley let a small smile escape. His reaction had been funny. Kiley leaned over and stole a deviled egg from the platter on his lap.

"Oh, Jane mentioned him. Isn't he some science geek?" Wade chimed in. There was no time for her to answer.

"How come he is not here spending Christmas with his girl?" Josh asked.

"Maybe he is scared of us," Wade offered.

"He is in L.A. with his family for Christmas."

"Ooooo, L.A.," they both hollered.

"Shhhh." Donna shushed them from the living room doorway, then disappeared again back to her bedroom.

"So, what is the story with you guys?" Kiley redirected the conversation. They both seemed jolly and inebriated. That made this the best time to get keep them talking, which was always entertaining.

"Us, no, we got nothing," Josh said. They both shook their heads in unison.

"You guys must have some great stories from growing up together. It must have been crazy. You guys didn't do anything dumb when you were teenagers?"

"Now, that is a totally different question," Wade replied.

"Did you guys ever get in trouble?"

"Every day," Josh said. They laughed together.

"Big trouble? Did you ever get arrested?" Kiley inquired, remembering what Miley had told her at the hospital.

"It was Wade's fault!" Josh yelled.

"It was ALL Josh's fault!" Wade shouted.

They pointed at each other. The baby started to cry upstairs.

"Oh. Now you've done it," Wade said and punched Josh. Josh punched him back. Wade flinched.

"So, what did you get arrested for?" Kiley asked, interested.

"Uh, the first time or the second time?" Josh asked. Wade punched him in the arm. Josh punched Wade back, this time in the chest.

"Does Jane know about this?" Kiley's voice went up an octave.

"She doesn't want to know these things. And people on the street do anyway," Wade reasoned, rubbing his chest with his hand where Josh had punched it. "Hell, Donna knows everything that goes on in this town, from dawn to dusk." They both chuckled. "If Jane wanted to know my indiscretions, she could just ask her. Kiley, you don't have to worry. Donna is a pretty good judge of character. If she thought I wasn't worthy of Jane, she wouldn't have let us get married," he finished.

"So? What did you guys get arrested for?"

"The one time, this buddy of ours—," Josh began.

"Yours," Wade corrected.

"This buddy was giving us shit."

"Doesn't sound like a buddy," Kiley said.

"Hey, if you want to hear the version I told the cops—"

"Lies," Wade coughed.

"YOU WILL QUIT INTERRUPTING ME," Josh said through gritted teeth.

"OK," Kiley agreed.

"For payback, we broke into his car, hot-wired it, and moved it somewhere he wouldn't think to look," Josh finished.

"Where did you move it to?" She was anticipating an answer like the barn or the ice cream shop or, at the worst, Huntington.

"The bottom of the pond," Wade finished, rolling his eyes.

Kiley gasped.

"Were you in big trouble?" she asked.

"With the law or my dad?" Josh answered a question with a question.

"I want to know both."

"Yes," Wade answered.

"But it wasn't as bad as the first time he had to bail us out of jail. Our dad expected it out of us by the second time," Josh bragged.

"He expected it of you. He couldn't believe I was stupid enough to follow you," Wade said, shaking his head.

"What did you do the first time?" Kiley was literally on the edge of her seat.

"I was mad at my English teacher, so we broke into the high school at night. The plan was to cover his classroom in shaving cream," Josh began

"That doesn't sound so bad," Kiley commented.

"Except it is breaking and entering no matter what you plan to do," Josh explained.

"And if you happen to accidentally break a window and start a fire while you are there, the cops and the principal get REALLY pissed," Wade said, giving the details to show the full picture.

"Oh my God, I remember when that happened! That was you guys?" Kiley was in awe.

"Hey, in our—"

"Your," Wade said.

"In MY defense, if there hadn't been a fire, we wouldn't have had to break the window to escape," Josh said.

"W-O-W," Kiley drew out the single syllable into three.

"Ya, so don't listen to that one. He is a bad seed," Wade pointed at Josh.

"Hey, I got us off easy. I gave a story about how we were acting out due to our dear mother's untimely death."

"You probably were," Wade said.

Josh just shrugged.

A few minutes later, Kiley headed to bed. Her two beers put her to sleep easily. But it made her have crazy dreams. Somehow her dream had Josh in an old James Dean movie in the actor's place. Kiley could only remember little images from the dream when she woke up. Josh in a leather jacket leaning against a classic car. How strange, she thought. All she knew about James Dean was that Jane used to have a picture of him in her bedroom.

12

JOSH

Josh put on a clean sweatshirt and put some gel in his hair, still damp from the shower. He made it do that stand up thing right in the middle in the front that all the girls like. He was about to head out with the rest of his family to the bar, the Broken Wheel, to have a few drinks and celebrate New Year's Eve. He had resisted the urge all day to ask Kiley if she would be joining them. It had its pros and cons either way. He desperately wanted her to come. But if she did, he couldn't flirt with her as openly as he had become accustomed in their late-night run-ins in the living room or the kitchen, when it was just the two of them. But even if he couldn't talk to her, just being able to look at her all night long would be better than nothing. He bet she had some cute little clothes in her closet to show off that hot bod. And if she didn't come tonight, he had no hope of seeing her tomorrow, as he had volunteered to work most of New

Year's Day at the convenience store, the Qwik Serv. He couldn't turn down holiday pay.

Just then he heard the door next to his room shut: Kiley's door. He hurried to run out and pass her in the hallway. It sure was convenient having her in the room next to his. Her door had swelled with all the humidity over the years, and she had to give it a real firm pull to get it shut. He just had to make sure he didn't find himself running out EVERY time he heard it, or she might catch on.

"Oh, hey. It looks like you aren't joining us tonight?"

Kiley was headed for the nursery, wearing her black pajamas with the pink skulls on them. They looked like an item she had probably bought at the little girl's goth store down at the mall.

"Ah, no. I'm gonna stay here and help Jane out with the baby."

"I bet Jane could handle the boy for a few hours on her own. C'mon, come."

"I don't mind," Kiley said. Except everything about the way she said it implied that she did mind.

"It might do you good to get out of this house. Join us. You don't know what you are missing," Josh boasted, letting his inner salesman out.

"I think I will be OK with just watching the big ball drop on TV."

"Well, if it's me you are worried about, my whole family will be there. That means I HAVE to be on my best behavior," Josh said, dropping his voice a little lower. He found himself smiling at her. He couldn't help it.

Kiley smiled back, her teeth glistening. Was he imagining it, or was there actually something between them? Her one crooked eye tooth peeked out from between her pouty lips. He loved that damn tooth.

"No. Thank you, though. Maybe next time." Kiley gave him a little wave, then went into the nursery. As Josh passed, he saw that Jane was already in there with Ethan.

So close. Close, but no dice. No one to kiss at midnight; at least not anyone he would be genuinely interested in.

KILEY

The week between Christmas and New Year's had gone fast. Kiley started doing some of the care of the baby. Since Jane had had a C-section, she needed more rest than for a normal delivery. Kiley supposed this was so that she wouldn't pop her stitches. Kiley liked that Jane needed more rest time. It gave Kiley more to do. Not only did it make her feel like she was not free-loading while staying with the Tuckers, it also gave her an excuse to procrastinate about her next book.

She got the email from Ted with the address to mail the books to, but he didn't write any more about his trip. And he never called her back. And now it was New Year's Eve. She knew he had returned to Georgia from his trip. She had held out hope all day that Ted would surprise her with a visit. But he hadn't even taken the time to call her. She had obsessively checked her phone all day long. She had checked it so much that she had drained the battery and had to put it on the charger by early evening, which she usually only had to do at bedtime.

Looking at the clock with the giraffe in the middle of it showing five minutes till midnight, Kiley had to admit the truth. He wasn't coming. He was probably partying with his friends back at school. And here Kiley sat, rocking her nephew in his nursery.

Everyone else in the house had gone to the Broken Wheel, except Jane, who was already asleep in the next room. The old house was kind of spooky when it was all empty at night. Kiley was glad Dave was laying in the doorway for protection from ghosts or the howling wind, even though Dave gave her a telling look that a potty break would soon be required.

Kiley sighed.

"I guess you are my New Year's Eve kiss, buddy," she said softly, and kissed Ethan on top of his peach-fuzzed head.

13

Kiley made a New Year's resolution: she would start her new book today. Or start the outline. Or brainstorm ideas. Or head to the grocery store to find the perfect notebook and pen to use to start it.

Kiley volunteered to take Jane to have her stitches removed just because she was a good sister. Nothing more. It wasn't because Kiley was going stir crazy in the house. Or that she was avoiding anything.

The Tuckers were all officially back to work after the holidays. This gave Kiley lots of opportunity to help Jane with the baby. And to start writing again. Definitely. Nothing spelled inspiration like a big, giant, quiet house all day long.

Hmmm. It was amazing how much time a newborn could suck out of your day. All that feeding and changing and bathing and napping. Not that Kiley was taking three hour naps herself. Never. There was work to be done.

It only seemed right if she was staying with the Tuckers that she should help with the housework, right? She was just being a good guest. Why else would she clean two and a half bathrooms whose frequent users included four men? Definitely not because of procrastination.

Kiley broke down and called Ted. They had a nice talk for over an hour. It was only after the call ended that she realized they had not made any concrete plans to visit one another. How had that happened? Weird.

Hmmm. There really wasn't much to do in Oakley. Especially if someone was trying to avoid something else. How had Kiley forgotten this aspect of her own hometown? What had she done when she lived here if she wanted to avoid homework? Could a twenty-two-year-old woman join the high school cheerleading team? Eh, probably not.

What day was it?

Kiley went to the library and visited the only copy of her book. She hid within the stacks and secretly autographed it.

Kiley received a call from the town library to kindly not deface any more of their books.

For something different, Kiley had dinner with Pete and Mackenzie at the Broken Wheel. The Broken Wheel was one of only two places to eat in town, and the only bar. She had thought about coming here since she had been back, just to get out of the house. Usually the place was so packed, like tonight, that if you came by yourself, you had to eat at the bar. So, she had avoided it. But it wasn't really that different than eating at the Tucker's. Donna brought the food to the table either way. And what was supposed to be so great about this place? Just because it was the only bar in town? Kiley used to want to come here at night unchaperoned by her parents so badly. Now she couldn't see what the draw had been.

Kiley stayed locked in her room all day (except for helping with the baby, of course) with only her notebook and her best writing pen.

At the end of the day, she had twelve pages of doodles to show for her time.

Kiley stayed locked in her room all day (excused from baby duty) with only her laptop.

At the end of the day, she had bought three new shirts, a pair of leather boots to match her new leather jacket she got for Christmas, a spork awesome enough to protect her from the next zombie apocalypse, and twenty five songs from SongTunz.

14

"How is the writing going? I mean I don't want to be nosy, I just wondered," Jane asked one day.

"Well, last night I wrote a poem about how my life is on hold until I can vomit some words out into the universe. Does that count?" Kiley replied, sarcastically.

"Well, if you are putting some words to paper, then it doesn't count as a total writer's block," Jane assured her.

"Thanks, I guess. I'm not sure my publisher feels the same way. I got an email from them this morning. They aren't even asking for an excerpt yet. They just want to know what my idea is. And I can't give them one."

"It will come. Maybe you just need to stop trying to force it. You came up with the idea for your first book while you were busy at the university. Maybe the key is to keep busy," Jane said, trying to be helpful.

"They say my name recognition is on an upward trajectory, and I need to make a follow-up before my post-tour dip gets too big. Whatever that means," Kiley frowned.

"I have an idea. Why don't you go down and help out in the farm office. You could just go down for a few hours a day. It would get your mind off of trying so hard to come up with an idea. Maybe you would find something that could inspire you," Jane said, smiling.

"Ya, maybe. Would that be OK? I mean, leaving you and the baby alone?" Kiley asked doubtfully.

"Of course. And you are all just five minutes away across a field."

"I guess you're right. Do you think it will be OK with Mr. Tucker? I don't have any 'skills.' "

"You can write and type and talk on the phone. I think you will be just fine," Jane reassured her.

"It would be nice to get out of the house, I guess," Kiley mumbled.

The next morning Kiley arrived at the office a few hours after everyone else. Evan seemed happy that she was there. He said that allowed him to go do more face-to-face marketing, like he could when Jane was tending to the customers. Kiley was pretty sure that meant go chat with the other farmers at the Diner while his wife served him a bottomless cup of coffee.

Kiley answered the few phone calls that came in. Most of them only wanted to talk to Evan, so she wrote down their names and numbers so he could reply upon his return. Someone called for Wade, so Kiley got to two-way him where he was out in the barn. That was different. Mostly, she was bored. Kiley knew Jane had her fingers deeper in the business than she herself would ever be as a temp.

Her notebook sat next to her, empty.

Once the Tucker boys all figured out Kiley was working there, they found it entertaining to pass through the office to bother her. Kiley found it both amusing and annoying at the same time. This was as close as Kiley would ever get to having brothers. She figured this was probably a pretty accurate representation. The worst one seemed to be Josh, though. He gave her the feeling of being a little girl in the schoolyard getting her pigtails pulled.

"Don't you have any work to do?" Kiley said to him, frustrated.

"Not really. It's winter. But don't tell my dad. I wouldn't want to get laid off or anything. I need the paycheck." Josh took another drink from the coke can that he had just grabbed from the office refrigerator. His hair looked disheveled, like he had been wearing a hat, but lost it in the few hours he had been at work.

"So you can buy more beer at the Broken Wheel?" Kiley accused.

"Something like that," he replied.

"Are you happy here in Oakley? To be a farmer all your life?" she asked him.

"Sure, I love it here, don't you?" he asked, surprised.

"It's too slow and quiet," Kiley answered.

"See, I agree. But if someone could bring a business in here to revitalize this area, bring jobs, it could change everything. It would draw more people to move to Oakley. Stores would be built for the people to shop at. Movie theaters and ball parks and other entertainment could follow." A light had appeared in his dark eyes.

"More likely Oakley will become a ghost town. It has been on that path for the last century. Every year there are just more empty storefronts and houses."

"Not if us Tuckers can help it."

"Well, I'm a writer. A career I can take with me anywhere," she stated.

"Funny, cuz I haven't seen you doing much writing since you got here."

Kiley reflexively looked down at her empty notebook, then scolded herself when she looked back up into his smiling face. She had given herself away. She could not deny now that his accusation held truth.

"It is called preparing. It's all up here," she pointed to her head, attempting a cover. He laughed, seeing right through her bluff.

Kiley had felt very fortunate to find her calling so early in life. Something that could make her money, and at the same time, it didn't feel like pulling teeth to get up out of bed and do it every day. No offense meant to dentists, of course. After all, Miley had spent years trying to find her purpose. Jane's profession mostly came out of convenience, as far as Kiley could tell. It got her college paid for by Mr. Tucker, and she was able to stay in Oakley with Wade.

'I found my way, but at the same time I have never felt so lost,' Kiley thought to herself. Everything in her soul pointed to the fact that she was destined to be a writer. But what if she wasn't good at what she loved? What if there were no future sales or success? What good was it to do what you loved, if that left you penniless and living on the street? Wouldn't that just make her a fool? She hoped Josh couldn't read all these thoughts as they passed across her face. The low-lidded gaze he shot her as he took a long swig out of the can told her otherwise.

Wade burst in just then.

"There you are, shithead. I've been looking all over for you. That equipment is heavy. We need all the help we can get to get it on the truck. I don't want to end up in the hospital with a hernia because you decided to take a coffee break," Wade chewed him out.

"Ya, ya," Josh said to Wade. He turned back to Kiley. "Duty calls. Now don't hurt yourself with all that 'preparing' now."

And they were gone. Oy. Maybe the key to getting inspired would be to leave boring old Oakley. But where would she go? She didn't have money for rent. Even if she wanted to move in with Ted, he would expect that much. Kiley wanted to avoid the drama she assumed was going on over at Miley's apartment. Her mother would probably let her stay for free, but she would also drive Kiley crazy. She had to stay here until she could provide enough of a story to receive her advance.

15

Kiley was up late again, waiting in the living room with *Third Shift* on low, her computer in her lap. Waiting? That wasn't the right word. What would she possibly be waiting for? Waiting for inspiration? Waiting to be tired enough for bed? Yes, that's what she told herself. The blackness outside the uncurtained kitchen windows told her it was very late, and that there was no moon out tonight.

She heard the front door open and shut. Her heart jumped in her chest. Dave's tail thumped on the floor across the room, although she made no move to get up. Kiley sat up straighter on the couch and stared more intently at her email.

"Hey, J.K. I heard you are off office duty," Josh crowed. His baseball hat was on backwards, the brown curls at the back of his neck peeking out below the rim. Guys at college wore their hats like that to try and look cooler. Back home in Oakley, it was much more natural; not a fashion statement. It was just a practical way to keep the sun off your head and the sweat out of your eyes while you worked. It was a good look on Josh.

"Ya, Jane was well enough to go back, and I wasn't helping you guys out that much anyway," Kiley replied.

"Oh, I don't know. I think some guys just stop in there to see the pretty girl that's working."

"I think some of those old farmers missed Jane a lot," Kiley replied.

"Ya, that Jane. She's a keeper... I heard there was pizza. Is there any left?"

"How did you hear that?"

"Wade told me."

"Oh. Well, he shouldn't have."

"And why not, Miss Rowling?"

"Because I finished it off."

"No way, you know you are supposed to save dinner leftovers for me."

"Well, then, maybe you should make it a point to be here for dinner."

"Not always possible."

Josh went into the kitchen. Kiley could hear him opening and closing the refrigerator door. He came out into the living room, and dropped himself next to Kiley on the couch.

"Funny how we keep running into each other like this," Josh said. He had a large turkey and ham sandwich on his plate.

He shoved a handful of potato chips into his mouth and crunched.

"Ya, I guess we are just two night owls."

"Lucky us. Hey, how is that story thing coming?" he asked, after swallowing.

"Oh, I sent my outline to my publisher. Now I just have to fill in two- to three-hundred pages of details," Kiley sighed.

"Good. You know, I thought it would be a lot more exciting living with a writer. Like, I thought Stephen King would be stopping by," Josh said before taking another bite.

"Ha, ha. I wish. I just lucked out with my first book. Maybe I am not cut out for this." Usually Kiley kept her guard up around Josh. But her disappointment in herself ran so deep now and yelled so loudly in her head, that it was escaping out in her words and into the world.

"Sure you are. You just don't need all the distractions of us running in and out of the house all day, throwing you off."

"No. That actually keeps it interesting," Kiley told him.

"Hey, you aren't writing about all of us, are you?" Josh gave a worried look. "Is it a tell-all? Wait! I know. This is one of those damn reality shows. I hate that shit! Where are the cameras? Tell me. Tell me!" Josh had worked himself up into a frenzy. He spun his head from side to side, looking up at the corners of the ceiling, then under the lampshade. Kiley was doubled over in laughter. She had to grab for her laptop at the last second to save it from crashing to the floor.

"No, not at all," Kiley said, wiping the tears of laughter from her eyes. "But you have given me a great idea!"

"Oh no. What have I done?" Josh screamed, throwing his hands up to his cheeks.

And then they laughed some more.

16

Kiley was in the kitchen grabbing a coke the next afternoon when the quiet house was suddenly filled with commotion.

"I can't believe you took the John Deere out of the barn and down to the south fields all day," Josh shouted as he followed Wade into the house, slamming the door behind them.

"It was equipment. I needed to use it," Wade shot back.

Neither brother realized she was a bystander to their disagreement, which had now moved into the living room. Donna was upstairs with Ethan. Josh and Wade were the first ones home for the day, both still in their work clothes that were caked in more dirt than usual.

"You knew I spent months shopping for a new one, because the old one was a piece of shit. Why wouldn't you think that I would want to be the first one to try it out?"

Kiley didn't know exactly what they were arguing about, but she could see Josh's face was blooming red as she peeked through the pass-through window undetected.

"Oh, listen to you. This is your 10-speed bike all over again!" Wade retorted.

"And you are still pulling the same crap 20 years later! You never learn."

"I had WORK to do."

"We all have work to do. And somehow you always end up with the easiest jobs and the best equipment," Josh declared.

"That's not true. We all rotate through the same jobs and you know it."

"Ya, and I always end up doing my share and yours. You know damn well that the work along Hallenback Road needs to be completed before the south fields. And you leave me with the old crappy one!"

"I'm sorry, sir. Is this a library? Do I have to check things out now? I didn't realize there was a pecking order for using the equipment. Make sure to leave a memo in my box about it." Wade waved his hands dismissively, heading upstairs.

"Dick," Josh called after him.

She thought Josh might come into the kitchen and discover her. Instead, he took off his baseball hat, running his hands through his hair with such pressure she was afraid he might rip it out. He exhaled, some of the crimson leaving his cheeks. Placing his hat back on, he turned and went outside. A moment later, his truck started and backed out of the drive. The tires spun in the gravel as he accelerated way too fast.

Donna entered the kitchen, Ethan in her arms.

"Have all the noisy boys cleared out?" she asked, handing the baby off to Kiley.

"I have never heard those two fight before."

"Oh, it goes in cycles. They will get along fine for a while. Then they will get into a tussle and not speak, which actually makes them even grumpier. They live in the same house and work at the same place. They use the same bathroom, for Pete's sake. No matter how mad they are, they can't escape each other. And they have no one to vent to because the man who serves that purpose is the one they need to bitch about."

"They will make up, right?"

"Oh, sure. Just give them a week or so."

Kiley didn't see Josh for the rest of the night.

17

Kiley received an email from Ted. She was excited to open it. He filled her in on how much homework his classes required and how he knew more than the professors teaching the classes. But instead of an "I love you" at the end, there was a request for another autographed book, this time personalized to a "Tiffahnie." Ugh. How many extra letters could someone pack into a relatively common name? Names like that were a pet peeve of Kiley's.

"So, like, what is the DEAL with your family?" Josh accused.

"What is the deal with yours?" Kiley shot back. She was sitting at the kitchen table having a before bed snack when Josh had arrived home. She was now on the verge of reverse-stalking him. Not following him, but waiting for him where she knew he would be. But they were all living in the same house, so it was kind of unavoidable. And not totally obvious.

He immediately began rummaging around in the refrigerator for food of his own. Kiley was beginning to wonder if the only meals he ate all day were breakfast and midnight snack.

"You know what I mean," Josh said.

"Do you always ask nosy questions of people you hardly know?"

"I know you. You have been living in my house for three months. I have seen you watch TV in your pajamas."

"You say that like they were revealing or something," she argued.

"Revealing is in the eye of the beholder," Josh said. Kiley arched an eyebrow in his direction. "So, reveal about your family," he continued. Josh placed a plastic wrapped plate of something into the microwave and set the timer. It hummed away in the background as he stood behind the chair at the table next to her. His hands were on the back of it, both his arms extended straight. Kiley thought she could detect the outline of his biceps through his flannel shirt. He continued to stare down at her, like a vulture on a power line, waiting for her answer.

"I don't want to."

"Didn't you put it all in your book or whatever?"

"You haven't read my book?" Kiley feigned shock. She really wasn't surprised at all.

"Not my style. But I heard that all the chicks really like it... Talk."

"You know, technically my family is your family, too. Jane is your sister-in-law," she pointed out.

"That makes me your, what? Brother-in-law-in-law?" Josh asked.

"Something like that..." Kiley knew the only way out of this was to leave and head upstairs, and she really wasn't ready to be alone again yet. "My family was, uh, distant growing up. We all lived in the same house, but we sort of all did our own thing. Sitting at the table and having a meal together was rare, only on holidays. My mom and dad never really shared with us what was on their minds. I don't know if other people's parents do—," she hesitated.

"They do, usually," Josh added.

"I mean, Miley and I were close. We shared a bedroom, we were in all the same sports and classes. But Jane sort of did her own thing. We didn't really get to know her until she left for college..."

"Miley's hot," Josh said.

"Shut up, you perv!" Kiley reached over and slapped his arm.

"I would do her."

"Ugh! God! We are like IDENTICAL twins. What does that say about me?"

"Ah, you got that weird, black, Morticia Addams hair going on," Josh said, wrinkling his nose and shaking his head. "I'm not into the goths."

"OMG, nobody calls it that anymore," Kiley rolled her eyes at him.

"OMG J.K., nobody says 'O-M-G' anymore," Josh rolled his eyes at her.

Kiley laughed, and threw a handful of crackers at him. He caught one and ate it. Dave cleaned up the remaining crackers off of the floor. The microwave alarmed its completion behind him, but he made no move to retrieve his food.

"So, like, you guys lived in the same house and didn't talk to each other or anything?" Josh returned to the original topic, apparently still curious.

"No, not like in this house. And we definitely didn't torture each other like you do to Wade. Hiding all the diapers on him was a very bad prank."

"Eh, it's all fun and games till the baby poops on him," Josh smiled that evil smile. The smile itself wasn't evil. But it showed all his straight white teeth. It curled up at the corners at a shocking angle that made him look like he was having mischievous thoughts. Which, knowing Josh, he probably was.

Josh remained standing there, looking at her. As his stare stretched into an uncomfortably long silence, Kiley decided ultimately that it was bedtime.

"Well, this bonding has been fun, but I'm heading to bed now," Kiley said, the wooden chair scraping the floor as she stood. Josh didn't miss a beat.

"That sounds like a good idea. I will come with you."

"You weren't invited," Kiley shot back.

"What do I have to do to get invited?"

"Grow up a little," Kiley retorted.

"Hmmm. I'm already nine years older than you. How old am I supposed to get?" Josh asked, cocking up his right eyebrow.

"Maturity and age are not inclusive."

"Exactly what I was thinking about you."

With that, Josh gave Kiley an accusing look. What he was accusing her of, she would probably never know. She pushed the swinging wooden door open and stepped through, holding it just long enough for Dave to follow.

JOSH

Josh's heart made an undetectable leap as he watched her walk out the wooden door of the kitchen. It continued to swing back and forth from her force, creaking slightly and spreading her girlie smell back at him. He remembered there was leftover lasagna in the microwave waiting for him, piping hot. As he stabbed it with a fork, he realized the top was rubbery and stiff from being over-radiated. He pulled out the chair he had been previously holding on to and sat in it. He stared at the now empty spot at the table Kiley had occupied, just a minute ago.

It seemed like he should be exhausted after working 16 hour days. And he was.

But immediately when he got home, he had this half hour of euphoria. He wasn't tired. Everything in his mind felt perfectly clear. Making plans to re-enforce his dream seemed easy. The ideas flowed. Then, well, he would crash. Wake up in the morning still wearing his clothes, while the obnoxious light still glared at him from the ceiling over his bed. All his brilliant ideas were forgotten, as he never thought to write any of them down.

Lately, he found himself using his midnight euphoria to harass Kiley. Sometimes he felt like maybe he was crossing a line. But she was always back again, almost every night, when he got home. He took that to mean that she wasn't offended. Heck, maybe she liked the sexual innuendos that he constantly threw at her.

Josh hadn't even been hungry tonight. He had eaten two trays of expired nachos at the convenience store before he left. But with Kiley munching in the kitchen, he took out some leftovers from the fridge, just to have an excuse to stay and talk to her longer.

She was different from her sister Jane. Jane came across as shy and weak, although they all had learned over time that she wasn't. When his dad left on vacation, Jane was supposed to be in charge of the business end of things, while Randy kept the employees in check, i.e. his brothers. But Jane always ended up having to crack the whip on all of them. Sure, they didn't like it very much. That is, until their dad came back. Then they missed having tiny little Jane with her hands on her hips boss them around.

Kiley wore strength on the outside, but inside she was still so young and naïve. Although, she had already seen way more of the country than Josh ever had. He worried that any day now, she would just up and leave. Load all her luggage back into her Toyota. Head back off to wherever she came from. It was his biggest fear. After all, it had already been three months. How long could someone continue to freeload in a house they had no real tie to? And she could literally move anywhere she wanted—she had said so herself. He was sure it would be somewhere far away where he wouldn't be able to make up an excuse to go visit her. But the thought of not seeing her for months, years was more than he could bear. It felt like a clock was counting down the precious moments he would have left to harass her. The thought of no more afterwork flirtations made his stomach cramp.

God, something about her had stolen his heart. And his dog. He wasn't sure that he could survive the first, and he wasn't real happy about the latter.

18

KILEY

Kiley was watching Ethan this afternoon. She had offered to pick up some groceries at the store for Donna. Donna was busy running from one job to the next. The least Kiley could do was try to multitask and be helpful.

Except, well, it was turning out that maybe babysitting and a quick errand like the grocery store were not activities that could be combined in any easy way. Kiley had put the formula powder and baby bottles of water into the diaper bag. She had taken it upstairs to add more diapers and wipes. She had dressed up Ethan in what she considered his cutest outfit, with the brown puppies on it. He had promptly wet through his diaper and, subsequently, the outfit. Kiley had changed him into one with frogs. Frogs were just not quite as cute. She had carried Ethan downstairs, along with a blanket, and carefully buckled him into his baby carrier. If she took Jane's car, it would snap right into the base. Ethan gurgled and wriggled happily in his carrier as Kiley found Jane's keys hanging on the key rack in the entryway. Kiley had found out soon after arriving that everyone left their keys there so that if a vehicle ever needed to be moved, the process would not require tracking down the owner.

At this point, Kiley realized she needed a few things of her own. She grabbed her purse and put the list Donna had made for her in it. She pulled her phone out of her back pocket to see if she had any new texts. None. And she was only a half hour behind on her mental schedule. She left it on the pass-through counter, next to the reusable bags Donna always took along.

Kiley had wanted to make it to the store before any of the family came home for lunch. She knew she would be rotten at getting all the necessary baby luggage together, but she wanted to try, and she didn't want anyone else interfering or looking over her shoulder. Especially Josh. He would sure have a smart-assed comment for her right about now.

Kiley looked around the living room. There was no sign of the diaper bag. She must have left it in the nursery.

"You hang tight, Ethan. I'll be back in a sec," Kiley said, running up the stairs.

Now that Josh had appeared into her head, she couldn't get him out again. His dark, chocolate brown eyes, his mischievous smile, and stubbly chin. He always looked like he had just rolled out of bed. He was definitely not someone that

Kiley needed to be filling up her subconscious with. But something about him drew her in. She could probably chalk it up to the fact that he was more of a challenge to Kiley—a happy challenge. More than Ted would ever be. Maybe she just liked Josh's flirty disposition. Perhaps it was just nice to think that possibly someone found her desirable. They were, admittedly, the only two single people living in the house. Wait, not single, per se. Unmarried, that is what Kiley had meant. That somehow allowed for Ted's involvement in her life. Yes. Ted.

Kiley could feel her face warming up. She rubbed her hand on the back of her neck. Her hand felt cold against the heat. It must have been the anxiety of the responsibility of taking the baby out by herself that had her overheated or the exertion of climbing the stairs. She looked in her bedroom, trying to remember what she had come upstairs for...

JOSH

Josh walked in the front door and kicked off his boots. He didn't even bother tying and untying them anymore. It was just easier to not bother. He tied knots in the laces so that they wouldn't fall off his feet completely at an inopportune moment. Lord knows his dad would start in on him about safety guidelines again.

He rounded the corner by the kitchen and almost tripped over little Ethan in his baby carrier. He had to grab onto the counter to steady himself, knocking a cell phone on the floor in the process. Ethan squealed at the action and smiled, spit running down his chin.

"Hey there, little guy. Now, who could have been so irresponsible as to leave you unattended like this?" Josh paused, looking around. "Me thinks it be the hot Kiley," he said to the baby.

He pushed Dave's nose out of the way and picked up the phone that was on the floor. The skulls on the case told him it was Kiley's. At that moment, a notification chimed from it. He pushed the button to illuminate the screen. He just wanted to see who the text had come from. The desktop picture was the cover of her book. Man, you would think that she would be tired of looking at that by now. The message icon was at the top. Without thinking, or while thinking very little, he quickly swiped the screen with his finger to unlock it. No luck; it required a 4-digit code. Josh tried Kiley's birth month and date. The screen immediately opened up to full function and brightness.

"Silly girl," Josh mumbled.

The message said it was from Ted. More specifically, it said:

From: <3 Ted

Josh found it hard to believe that anyone would "heart Ted," let alone Kiley. She was such a colorful girl. Well, not in the clothing sense. She actually wore a lot of black. But her personality was so...vivacious. Ted always seemed like a real dud, from what Josh had gathered. He hazarded a glance at the base of the stairs. No black-haired pixie was bouncing down. Maybe he should just see what this Ted had to say...

KILEY

She had decided to grab a toy to entertain Ethan while he would be riding around in the shopping cart at the store. She hooked the now heavy diaper bag over her shoulder and headed downstairs. Turning the corner to proceed into the living room and toward Ethan, Kiley stopped short. She wasn't entirely surprised to see someone home for lunch already. But she was instantly furious to see him messing with her phone. She ran up to him and yanked it out of his hand.

"What the FUCK do you think you are doing?" Kiley screamed at the same time, making Josh visibly jump.

"I was going to take goofy pictures with your camera. Maybe some down my pants," he replied, never missing a beat.

"Then why is my screen showing text messages?" Kiley shoved the phone in his face to prove her point.

"I must have gotten lost. My phone isn't this fancy."

"How did you even get passed my security code?" she asked, realization dawning on her face even before she finished the sentence. "You hacked my phone!"

"Maybe you should take it as a lesson to invent a more secure password."

"You asshole!" Kiley pushed him, hard in the chest. She expected to push him backwards, at least to make him sway. But his body didn't move an inch.

"Hey now," Josh purred to her, putting his hands up in the air jokingly, as if she was wearing a slutty policewoman Halloween costume and pointing a Hello Kitty bubble gun at him. It pissed her off even more, so she pushed him again. Dave jumped up on her and barked. It was a warning. Apparently Josh was still where her ultimate canine loyalties lay. Ethan began to cry. He probably had the scariest vantage point, being on the floor, looking directly up at all the chaos.

"Knock that off!"

"You think this is funny? I don't think that invasion of my privacy is funny! I do business with this phone. What if you deleted something from my agent or my publisher!"

"I wasn't deleting anything!"

Kiley looked at her phone for the first time. "No, but it looks like you were reading things. Why are you so obsessed with Ted? Are you looking for sexting pictures? Do you have a thing for guys or something? Is that why you don't have a girlfriend?"

"You don't know anything, little girl, and I recommend you stop talking right now." All the wrinkles on Josh's forehead lined up to make a disapproving "V."

"I know I am sick of you and your smart mouth butting into my business."

"Whatever. You are the one that is staying at my house, J.K."

"And stop FUCKING calling me that!"

"Kiley! What's going on here?" Wade asked, as he and Pete came through the entryway, his eyes open wide. Luckily, Mr. Tucker and Randy were still approaching the door from the driveway, so they missed the show.

"I hate you!" Kiley screamed, then slung her purse and the diaper bag over one arm, and the baby carrier over her other. Everything else she had gathered was left behind as she stormed out the door to Jane's car.

And even in that moment, as mad as Kiley was at him, she knew that deep down, she didn't really hate Josh. She hated herself because she couldn't stop thinking about him.

19

Kiley hadn't talked to Josh for a week since the fight over him snooping through her phone. She wasn't really avoiding him. But she wasn't making a point of being in common areas of the house at times when she knew he was around, either. She was reverse anti-stalking him. It gave her a sense of satisfaction to make her point about how big of an infraction it was by withholding her presence from him. But, well, it also made her life much less entertaining. The days went slower when she didn't have at least one daily verbal sparring match with Josh. And she wondered if he even noticed at all. Maybe he had stayed out later than usual these past nights and had not even noticed her absence. What if she was really only torturing herself?

Her words still being held captive by the dark mistress Writer's Block, Kiley had to find a way to break them free. She hoped a change of scenery would do the trick. Not having any baby duty today, Kiley packed a tote bag filled with her notebook, two pens (in case one went dry), a novel, and a non-refrigeratable lunch. Kiley knew what was most likely to get used out of the bag, and what contents were most likely to be left in there until she returned once again to the house. But she figured she could deal with her guilty conscience later.

Kiley walked through the short rows of the crops that were beginning to sprout in the fields. She had no idea what type of plant it was at this stage. Kiley could only identify them at harvest time. Farming had never been her forte.

It had never been her "field" of expertise.

She laughed at her own pun.

She tried to clear her mind as she trudged through the muddy soil. It didn't work. Her brain was too clouded and there were a few lakes of standing water she had to detour around. She was wearing old sneakers, but that was no reason to trash them completely. Why did it have to rain so much in spring, anyway? The clouds that were presently rolling in from the west actually looked like they could be bringing more precipitation. Maybe today had been a bad choice for a field trip. She should have checked the weather forecast first.

As she was already heading in that general direction anyway, Kiley decided the main barn might be a good place to hang for the day. Once she arrived, she almost changed her mind. There were a number of livestock housed in the building, and their smell was pushing any creative thoughts out of her head. Or, at least that is the excuse she fed herself.

Rounding a corner into another area of the barn where the tools, shovels, wheelbarrows, etc. seemed to be stored, Kiley had to muffle a surprised shout when she happened across someone else in there with her. Josh lay in a pile of hay and horse blankets, snoring. He was freakin' sleeping in the barn! Kiley chuckled. She actually counted herself lucky. If she had stumbled upon him awake, they would have either had to make up or continue their fight. It was easier this way. She could just sneak away, and he would never know that she had been here. Except, well, Kiley didn't find herself leaving.

Instead, she moved closer and knelt down, watching the even intake and exhale of his breathing. He had a baseball hat on that had been knocked askew in his sleep. She studied how the dark stubble grew through his skin. She could tell where he shaved it and where he didn't to achieve his signature "I don't care" look. She saw where a few gray hairs were mixing in. Her hand reached to touch his cheek, but she stopped herself and quickly pulled it away. He was different like this. She was used to his piercing dark eyes, his electric wit sparked by his gravelly voice, and his evil smile being his most outstanding features. Laying here like Sleeping Beauty, they were all non-existent. Kiley couldn't help being drawn to him, but she had no idea why.

She stood back up. She was going to leave the barn, but she could hear a steady rain now hitting the roof. Maybe they could both hide out here from the world, and each other. There had to be enough space out here in this old barn. Kiley did another pass, then found the ladder that led up into the hayloft. She found herself a cozy spot and settled into it. She pulled the book out of her bag first. She wasn't excited to read it, but it was on her list of classic books to read as "research"—to be a more well-rounded person and better writer. Although it would be a challenging book, she knew reading would be much easier than pulling words out of thin air for her own writing.

As the rain strummed steadily above, Kiley began to wonder if she might nod off as well.

JOSH

"God dammit, Josh! Get your ass up! I don't pay you to sleep!" the most annoying voice in the universe awakened Josh. He rolled over, pushed off the blanket, and sat up, still not making eye contact with his father.

"Josh, you fell asleep on the job. I can't ignore that, son."

"C'mon. Cut me a break," Josh pushed the words out of his sore throat. Trying to rub the sleep out of his eyes, he realized how foggy his brain was, and knew he must have been asleep for quite a while. He had only meant to rest his eyes for a minute or two. He had started coming down with something last night, but had gone to work at the Qwik Serv anyway. Sore throat, headache, stuffed up nose, possibly even a little fever. No doubt from working in the rain these past few days. As Josh looked over his father's shoulder out the open barn door, he could see that today would be no different. He grabbed his baseball hat and put it back on his head to cover his dirty hair. He was in no condition to shower this morning. He pulled the bill low, so as to have as little eye contact with his angry father as possible. He tried to power through his sickness this morning, just to not have to hear his dad's shit about calling off, but, well, shit, here he was listening to it anyway.

"No. When are you going to learn to take work seriously?"

"This speech again," Josh grumbled. There was no point in telling his dad he was ill. It would just be seen as an excuse. And excuses were unacceptable, as Josh had been told over and over again.

"Again? Does that mean that you actually heard it all those other times I have recited it to you? Does that mean that you just chose to ignore it?"

"It means I do the best that I can."

"And sleeping on the job is the best that you can?"

"Dad, this is OUR farm. It is not a factory busting out car parts. I could have gone up to the house and taken a nap in my own bed if I was going to blatantly disobey you."

"You have that wrong, son. It is MY farm, until the day I die. I should boot your ass out of here and you can go work at an auto factory. You wouldn't last a day. Your sense of entitlement is going to bite you in the ass one of these days."

"My sense of entitlement! I am fuckin' workin' two jobs for—," Josh stopped, censoring his statement. He was so frustrated that he was doing all this hard work, and couldn't share it with anyone. His father would just continue to see Josh as the goof-off son as he always had.

"Ya, son, for what? Why exactly is it you think you need to work two jobs? Do you think I don't pay you enough?"

"No Dad, that isn't it."

"Then what? Because I am tired of paying you to perform a job that you are too tired to do cause you spend half the night selling cigarettes and slushies? I think you should quit that job."

"What? You think that you can dictate my life just because you are my father?" Josh asked, beyond irritated.

"And your boss. I think you forget that."

"You don't see me as an employee. You never have. You see me as your worthless son." He couldn't keep it bottled up any longer.

"If the shoe fits."

"That shoe doesn't fit, D-A-D. Down at the store, they think I'm a good employee. They offered to make me assistant manager, but you know what? I didn't take it. The hours would conflict with my work here on the farm."

"Then go, be their junior manager. I don't need you around here."

"I would, if I didn't need the money..." Josh could have kicked himself. It must be all this snot clogging up his head. He had almost given away his plan twice during the same conversation. And he couldn't be fighting with his dad when he told him. Not in the middle of one, anyway. He needed his Dad's cooperation to get the land that he needed for the project. He also needed two incomes to save up for his share.

"Back to this again. What do you need money so bad for, son? Are you in trouble? Gambling, drugs?"

"Oh right, of course. Josh must be in trouble. Because that is all you see in me."

"Because that is all you have ever shown me."

'I'll show you,' Josh thought but did not say out loud, as his dad turned and stormed out. Josh couldn't wait to be his own boss. He would have his own employees someday, and he definitely wouldn't treat them like this. He turned his hat around backwards, so that he could see better in the dim light of the barn.

Josh turned, and caught sight of unmistakable black hair ducking around the corner.

"Kiley?" He was still so mad from his discussion with his father that he didn't even remember to tease her with the dumb nickname.

"Um...ya?" she mumbled, walking out from behind the wall to face him. She looked up at him from under her thick eyelashes and black eyeliner, their small height difference more noticeable than the times when they were in the house sitting on the couch.

"You didn't by any chance hear all that, did you?" Josh could barely ask her. He was so embarrassed. He always wanted to present himself as a big macho guy in front of her. Now she had heard him be reamed out by his dad like a tiny child who had just wet his pants.

"Well, a little... I mean, I didn't want to. But there didn't seem to be a good way to leave without, you know, interrupting," Kiley paused. They just stood and looked into each other's eyes. "I mean, he was really pissed at you. I didn't want him to be mad at me too."

Josh chuckled, but it didn't reach his eyes. "Good point. I wouldn't want him to threaten to harm a pretty little hair on your head."

"Would he do that? I mean, use violence?"

"No. He got in a few fist fights at the bar before we were ever a glint in his eye, but he prefers to just use verbal abuse on his own family."

"Does he talk to all of you like that?"

"When we were young, yes. But Mom always acted as a buffer. Then, well, after my mom passed, he picked favorites. Somehow, Wade and I got the short end of the stick."

"After the stories you told me on Christmas," Kiley proceeded quietly and cautiously, "I think you guys may have given him a reason to."

"Well, I get why you would say that. I'll admit, our wild streaks run deeper than Randy and Pete, but they were no angels either. And, well, when someone tells you over and over that you are dumb and a troublemaker, at some point, you just start to believe them."

"I'm sorry," Kiley cooed. Tears threatened to spill out of her honey eyes.

"Ain't nothing for you to be sorry for," Josh reasoned, fighting back his own tears now.

Then Kiley closed the few feet between them and wrapped her arms around him. It surprised him, but he wrapped his arms around her as well, letting his head rest on top of hers. He took the opportunity to bury his nose into her dark hair and inhale her scent. They stood like that for several minutes. He felt like he was gaining strength from her.

"Hey, Josh, ya in here?" Wade's voice called from the front door.

Kiley and Josh jumped apart.

"Ya. Right here," Josh replied, ducking his head down as he composed himself. He rubbed his hand under his nose.

"See ya later," Kiley squeaked out, as she headed for the door, passing Wade. He knew Wade would be ready with a smart comment. He saved it for Josh.

"You gettin' some action, brother?"

"No, no way. Not today."

Kiley flipped up the hood on her jacket and walked out into the drizzle, her bag hanging at her side.

"Man, we gotta go out and do something tonight. Today has been a shitty day."

20

Kiley was sitting on the couch with the TV remote control in her hand. It would be dinnertime soon. Another common, ritual event to move the day along. Her spiral-bound notebook and pen were within reach, but were cast aside. Kiley had come to realize that she had no interest in writing the story to flesh out the outline she had already submitted to her publisher. But it had bought her time.

She wasn't even attempting to fake working on her book anymore. She had zero motivation. Her limbs felt like they were made of cream cheese, too heavy to move, too weak to support her. It was very possible that her first book had just been a fluke. What if she couldn't duplicate its success? Maybe she would never have another creative idea that she could expand into 80,000 words ever again? She was beginning to feel like an all-out failure. She was like a clock hanging on the wall whose battery had run so low that it kept ticking, but no longer had the force to push the second hand up over the number twelve any longer; she was trying, but getting nowhere.

Wade and Josh stumbled down the stairs. Wade was in front, but Josh pushed him from behind. Then Wade turned around and pushed Josh back. Wade began laughing, Josh only made had the slightest hint of a smile. Kiley hoped the baby was not trying to sleep as their feet thundered on the steps. It was as if the expression "like a bull in a china shop" had been invented just for them.

For the moment, it seemed as though Josh had mostly recovered from his earlier incident with his father. At this point, Kiley had no idea where her and Josh stood. They had been buddy-buddy, then she had flipped out when he snooped in her phone. Then she had watched him be utterly humiliated. She had, well, comforted him (is that what that was?), then ran out of the barn. She wasn't even sure if he would want to talk to her ever again. She stayed where she was on the couch, trying to be small and inconspicuous.

"So where do you want to go tonight?" Wade asked, grabbing one of the small apples out of the fruit bowl in the pass-through. Wade shoved it in his mouth and took a bite that was almost half the size of the entire apple.

"I have a few ideas," Josh replied, rounding the corner into the entry way and grabbing his jacket. As he spun to put it on, he saw Kiley on the couch.

"Hey, uh, we are headed out. Wanna come with?" Josh asked her, his mouth hanging open slightly, accentuating his bottom lip.

"Uh, I don't know. Can I?" Kiley was unsure. It seemed like they were on the verge of brother bonding. She didn't know if she would ruin their party.

"It's OK with you, man, right?" Josh turned, looking to Wade.

"Oh, ya, she's cool," Wade's blond eyebrows bounced up as he answered Josh. "She does know how to keep a secret, right?" Now Wade's blue eyes were trained on Kiley. She looked to Josh, whose dark eyes met hers. She saw that the twinkle had returned to his eyes.

"I don't know, can you?" Josh challenged her.

"Miley still doesn't know why her fingernails fell off senior year."

"Oooh, I think she's good," Wade crowed.

"Yes, you're in. C'mon. Grab your coat," Josh said. Kiley bounced off the couch, leaving her notebook behind. There was nothing in it for anyone to read anyway. As she approached the entryway between Josh and Wade, Josh put his hand on her back on her way by. It was out of the ordinary, but seemed natural and comforted her.

"Why do I need my coat? It is warm outside." The rain had happily ended around noon and the sun had busted out for the rest of the day, making a wet haze hang heavy in the air.

Even with the rain stopped, there were sure to be puddles and mud. She slipped on the old boots that Jane had given her, rather than her shoes, which were still wet and muddy from earlier. Kiley thought of them as her "muck boots."

"Not where we are going, honey." Josh winked at her.

She was tired of being called J.K., but honey didn't seem any better. Kiley was a little nervous as she walked out the door at the mercy of the two brothers who once set fire to the school.

After stops at the hardware store and the grocery store, Kiley found herself following Josh and Wade through a field of tall, unmowed grass on the edge of town. The sun had set before they had parked Josh's truck. Kiley had sat squeezed in-between the two men. Growing up in the country, Kiley had found herself squeezed three- or four-wide in a pickup truck many times, usually after school or football games. It had been years. She couldn't help but think Josh might be enjoying it a little more than he should.

"C'mon, kid. Quit your lollygagging back there and keep up!" Josh yelled. He and Wade had gotten a distance ahead of her with their long legs in the tall underbrush.

Kid. So maybe Kiley was reading too much into everything. Maybe the hug this afternoon, the hand on her back at home, and the snugness of the truck ride were all in her imagination. He did see her as just a kid. Jane's kid sister. That was probably why he was nice to her. Probably the only reason why he kept her company at night when he got home. After all, he was 31 and she was only 22. She jogged to catch up. Why were these thoughts in her head? She was being silly. Josh was probably that flirty with all the girls. She must just be desperate for some male attention. She would have to call Ted when she made it home.

"Where are we going, anyway? There is nothing out here but the water tower," Kiley asked when she caught up and walked between them.

They looked past her at each other and smiled.

"Hope you aren't scared of heights, Miss Rowling," Josh looked at her with his wide evil smile.

"You have to be joking." That is, she would call Ted IF she made it home alive.

"Now J.K., I am not jk."

"You aren't scared of heights, are you? I don't want you puking or falling off or anything," Wade said, trying to be considerate, but pretty much failing.

"No, I should be fine. Hopefully." They walked further, the water tower looming closer and closer above them. "You guys aren't planning on pushing me off when I get up there, are you?" Kiley asked worriedly, as she looked up at the tall silver water tower that resembled the tin man from *The Wizard of Oz*. It announced to everyone that they were in fact in the Village of Oakley.

"No way, J.K. I don't think you would make a very pretty splatter," Josh replied, as they reached the base of the water tower. Kiley had spent more time with Josh, but somehow she would have felt more comforted if Wade had been the one to reassure her. Josh jumped up to reach the bottom rung and hauled himself up the ladder.

"Uh oh, looks like I'm too short. I'll have to wait for you guys down here," Kiley yelled to him.

"Oh, plenty of girls have come up here with us. We know they always need a boost," Wade said, at the same time he grabbed her by the waist and lift her up, so that her hands were nicely at the bottom rung. Kiley took a hold of it, knowing she did not have the upper body strength to haul herself up.

"But, I can't..."

Wade interrupted her.

"Now, put your feet on my shoulders. There you go. Now you can use your feet to sort of boost yourself up. That's it."

Kiley's heart banged against her rib cage as she began her ascent up the tiny ladder to the top of the water tower. She didn't know why she was surprised. When she had agreed to head out with them, she knew the night would be eventful.

As she tried to raise each boot to continue upward, it always seemed like the rubber would pass against the rungs, causing a drag and slowing her down. Josh was quite a ways ahead of her. Kiley would look up every now and then to try to gauge the distance. The dark green backpack he wore bounced on his back as he took one rung after the next. She could tell that his jeans were riding down as he climbed. Kiley wanted to look down and see how close Wade was behind her, but then she would know how high they were, and she didn't want to fathom that.

Kiley realized Josh had stopped, although they were only halfway up.

"Why are you stopping?" she asked him, a slight panic escaping in her voice. Her muscles burned with exertion.

"Duh. I have to cut the lock." With one leg looped around the ladder, he managed to get a set of bolt cutters out of his backpack.

"But then people will know someone was up here."

"Oh, trust me. They are GOING to know."

Kiley heard Wade's chuckle just below her in the darkness.

"So this wasn't just a spur of the moment thing? You planned to come up here all along?" There was a loud snap.

"Best place in town to be quiet and think. Plus, after years of getting drunk and climbing this far only to realize we forgot the tool, we know better now."

"Ya, only took us like 10 years," Wade said.

There was a second loud snap, this time something fell past them, hitting the metal ladder and clanging as it hurtled to the earth at the mercy of gravity.

"Thanks for the warning," Wade muttered to Josh.

"What were you going to do? Jump out of the way?"

Josh swung open a gate that had been covering a large portion of the stairs, and continued to climb. Kiley followed. There was more wind the higher they went. She was glad she had worn her jacket. Kiley couldn't wait until she got to the top where she could zip it up.

There was the loud whine of metal scraping against metal as Josh opened some sort of door, then disappeared from sight.

"Josh?" she called out.

"Keep climbing, J.K. You're almost here."

"Where's 'here'?"

"The top."

There was now metal over Kiley's head like an overhang or roof. She could feel herself slowing down. Her arms and legs felt like jelly from all the climbing. She saw the tiny rectangle that was only three rungs above her head. There was no way she was going to make it.

Then two arms reached through the opening and hauled her up. She laid there for a second, trying to catch her breath.

"How out of shape are you, kid?" he said, but she could tell his breathing was just now normalizing as well.

"Scoot over so I can get up, people," Wade griped loudly. Josh grabbed Kiley by her jacket and pulled her far enough away from the opening so that Wade could get up.

"Man, you guys are rough," Kiley whined.

"Oh, you have no idea—," Josh began.

"Behave," Wade cut him off.

Josh helped Kiley to her feet.

"Oh my God, the view up here is so beautiful—" The words caught in Kiley's throat as she looked out on the lights of their tiny town spread out before them.

"It makes the town look even smaller than it already is," Josh said, as he rummaged through the backpack. Wade settled himself on the brink of the platform, hanging his feet off the edge to dangle, his chest leaning against the lowest part of the railing. Josh handed him a glass bottle of beer, a submarine sandwich, and a full size bag of potato chips.

"Dude, why did you bring glass? Cans would have been lighter," Wade asked him.

"Store didn't have the kind we like in cans. The liquid is the heaviest part, either way," Josh replied.

Kiley carefully sat down in the same fashion that Wade had. He ripped open the bag of chips and offered them to Kiley. She took a handful. All the exercise had left her famished.

"Here," Josh said, handing her a beer and a sandwich. He had already removed the cap for her.

"What kind is it?" Kiley asked as she opened the white paper wrapped around the sub.

"Don't worry, it's what you like. I have lived with you all this time, I think I know what you eat."

"Oh, well. Thanks." It was a turkey sandwich, topped with only cheese, lettuce, banana peppers, green peppers, and jalapenos. Josh took a seat on the other side of Wade. They ate and drank in silence until the sandwiches were finished.

"You know, Josh, I am not climbing up here with you every time you have a fight with Dad."

"Ya, I know. I just needed some distance tonight is all."

"Well, the next time try using your truck for that. You can always head on up to the strip club in Parker," Wade smiled at Josh. He didn't seem to find the joke amusing. Josh pulled out another beer, offering it to Kiley. When she declined, he opened it for himself and took a long swig.

"You can't let dad get under your skin. He had you and me stereotyped years ago, and nothing is going to change that now."

"I don't know. Your little husband and wife and baby thing you and Jane got going on, that seems to have humbled him some."

"Maybe. But he still sees me as an irresponsible kid as long as I am under his roof. I can't wait till our house is done."

"But I can't move out."

"Why not? You are working two jobs, you must have some money stashed away."

Kiley wondered why every conversation today mentioned that.

"I can't, man. I'm... I'm just saving. I just need more time."

"Dude, you're over 30. It's time to shit or get off the pot."

"Ya, I guess," he replied. Josh was quiet for a while. The wind whistled past them. The moon began to rise up into the sky. If Kiley squinted, she felt like maybe she could actually see it as it moved.

"Are you tired of hearing the Tuckers' dirty laundry today?" Josh sniffed.

Only then did Kiley realize Josh had been quiet because he had been crying. She wanted to hug him again, as she had earlier in the barn. But she didn't make a move to. She couldn't read the tone of his statement. Was he mad that he had asked her to come along? Was he trying to lighten the mood? She wasn't sure.

"Just family stuff. Everyone's got it," she replied. The end of her statement got whisked away into the night. There was more silence. Kiley spoke up about what had been on her mind since they had first started their climb. "Wade, you said you had brought chicks up here before. Did you ever bring Jane up here?"

"Oh, I knew better than to ask her. She wouldn't be down for this sort of thing."

"I think you should ask her sometime. It is beautiful up here."

"You don't think she will think we are pathetic for being old guys and still climbing the water tower?"

"I don't think that. She has a wild streak. She married you. And then you went and got all boring on her," she accused.

"Is that how you see it?"

"Yes."

"Is that how JANE sees it?" Wade asked worriedly.

"I don't know. I have never asked her. Maybe you should," Kiley answered.

"Maybe I should."

"I told you not to marry the brain in town. Man, she sucked all the fun out of you," Josh said.

"Hey, man, I agreed to come up here tonight, didn't I?"

"So, wait. You want your dad to see you as more grown up, yet you keep doing stuff like trespassing on the water tower?" Kiley asked.

"I am trying to cut down, believe me. And we didn't come all the way up here just to trespass."

As Kiley looked at Josh, puzzled, he produced a can of black spray paint from the backpack. He began to shake it, the ball rattling rhythmically inside with his motion.

"Vandalism! What happens if we get caught?" Kiley exclaimed.

"That's why we come in the dark," Wade leaned over and drawled into her ear. "You act like it is a surprise that we can climb tall things and paint graffiti. You have seen Jane's wedding proposal."

"Oh ya," Kiley replied.

"So, what are you going to paint, big brother."

"Not sure yet. Maybe a personal attack."

"Not on your Dad!" Kiley cried.

"I'm all for vandalism, but not for excommunication from my town," Josh answered. "That man is a saint around here."

"Then who?"

"Who's that guy who never calls or visits you?" Josh asked Kiley.

"My dad?" she replied.

"Funny. No, the other one."

"My boyfriend."

"Doesn't sound like much of a boyfriend to me," Wade said. "He doesn't mind you living in a house full of guys?"

"I don't think I ever told him. He never asked."

"What's his name?"

"Ted."

"Well, Ted sucks," Josh stated bluntly.

"I think you got yourself some graffiti, brother."

Josh shook the paint can, then shoved it into a pocket on his jacket. "If you were mine, I'd...," he began, the clanging of his feet on the ladder drowning out the rest of his statement as he ascended.

21

Kiley woke up with the sun streaming through a crack in her curtains and a throbbing headache. She rolled over to get out of bed, but was confronted with the worst soreness she had ever known in each and every limb. She tried to get up again and knocked a beer bottle off her nightstand and onto the floor instead, hitting her toe.

"Ah, shit." That hurt. Kiley contemplated which would make her feel better, a shower or breakfast. Just then a knock sounded at the door.

"Kiley, are you awake?"

"Sure, Jane, come in," she answered weakly, knowing she would come in anyway.

"I wanted to remind you that we are going out with Mom and Miley tonight. Don't forget to wear something nice."

"Oh, that's tonight? OK." The days of the week were all blending together.

Jane began to shut the door, then popped back in.

"You will never guess what happened last night. Someone spray painted graffiti on the town water tower. It has a crude drawing of a penis and it says "Ted sux." Who would DO such a thing? And it is such a weird coincidence that that happens to be your boyfriend's name. Weird," she muttered as she shook her head and left the room.

Now memories of last night flooded back to Kiley. Jane had no clue it had indeed been for her Ted. She held out her hand like a girl with a new manicure coming straight from the salon, but instead of nails, she was admiring the splatters of black paint that clung to her hands. The painting was Josh's handiwork, but she had been in the splatter zone. There was something redneck chivalrous about his efforts.

Jane and Kiley went to Huntington, to visit their mother, aunt, and sister. They went to dinner at a nice restaurant, and then went to see a musical. Everyone else had heard of it except Kiley. She usually at least knew the most general of information about an entertainment release, thanks to her subscription to ShoBiz Weekly. But she had been a bit out of touch for the past year, ever since she BECAME part of the entertainment industry. Someone at the show recognized her from a picture in the newspaper during intermission.

"Oh, I just loved your book. You are from the area, right?" the woman asked. It was always women. Apparently Kiley's book repelled men. Hey, maybe there was a new book idea somewhere to be found in that thought.

"Yes, I was raised right down the road in Oakley."

"Oh, then why did you ever set your book in Michigan, dear? I grew up in Michigan and you got the weather all wrong in your book."

"Oh, well, thank you for the feedback," Kiley stuttered, struggling to keep her words polite. If this woman was just going to be disparaging, why had she interrupted Kiley's evening with her family. There were people who got paid to pick her book apart—they were called critics.

"It's not feedback, honey. You wrote it all wrong. You had Monica in a sleeveless dress with no coat in January. Her arms would have turned blue and fallen off."

"It was my understanding that Michigan weather could vary greatly in the same day, and all year long. I found data that the record high for January 2nd was 62 degrees. Plus, if you'll remember in the book, there was magic in the air that night..."

At this point, Miley dragged her sister away from the woman and back to their seats. The woman was still explaining to her friends all the inaccuracies in the book.

"It's fiction," Kiley told her sister.

"I know," Miley consoled her.

"I could have it rain candy if I wanted to."

"I know," Miley echoed.

"I could have a herd of unicorns stampede through the village to eat the candy."

"Shhh." Miley's patience had come to an end as the lights dimmed in the theater.

They got back home late. Jane went upstairs right away to check on the baby and turn in for the night. Kiley changed into her pajamas, then went back downstairs to wait. Dave gave her a dirty look when Kiley began to walk out of the bedroom. Dave had already curled herself up into a ball on her dog bed and was clearly ready to call it a night.

Kiley had never had a dog before. It was really great, but also a lot of work. A lot like a newborn baby. Maybe Kiley shouldn't have started caring daily for both species at the same time.

"Stay, if you want," Kiley told her, heading out the door.

With a groan of disgust, Dave stood, stretched, and followed her downstairs. Kiley hadn't waited up for Josh in a week, but after everything they had gone through the day before, she felt she owed it to him. And she wanted to see what his attitude would be like. The musical had been good enough, but being around all those stuffy people in their fancy clothes and big opinions just made Kiley want to be herself and shoot the bull with Josh. She had missed him all night. It wasn't any later than usual, but Kiley was so tired, she fell asleep on the couch in minutes.

When she woke up the next morning, someone had covered her with one of the blankets that were kept on the quilt rack in the living room for cool evenings. Dave was lying on the other couch. Somehow she was still looking at Kiley with that same disgusted stare. Apparently Dave was not a girl who liked changes in her routine.

"Go back to Josh, then," Kiley told her out loud.

Dave only blinked in reply.

Kiley saw very little of Josh during the next week. He seemed to always be out or sleeping. The single night that their paths crossed, he seemed happy enough to see her.

"Hey, J.K. Climb any more water towers since I've seen you last?" he smiled widely at her as he hung up his coat and keys. He patted Dave's head as she sniffed him.

"Have you committed any more acts of vandalism?" Kiley said from her perch on the couch.

"I plead the fifth."

"I am sure that you do."

"By any chance, you weren't waiting up for me now, were you?" Josh walked over closer to her, but made no move to take a seat on the couch.

"No, never," Kiley snorted. Her denial may have been too emphatic. "I just wanted to watch this episode of *Timmy Killon*."

"Right. Only teenagers obsessed with movie stars and old people who can't sleep watch those programs," Josh pointed out. Dave stood at the bottom of the stairs, waiting for SOMEONE to head to bed.

"Maybe I'm a teenager at heart."

"Now that you brought it up, didn't you used to be a cheerleader?"

"Ya, when I was like 16. Miley and I both were. Do I not seem like cheerleader material?"

"Both of you? Dang. Twins in cheerleading uniforms. Did you do those little flips that showed your underpants?"

"Shut up!" Kiley yelled at him.

"Do you still have your uniform?" Josh asked, his mouth open, his bottom lip hanging down again, drawing Kiley's attention.

"You will never find out! And it wouldn't fit anymore anyway."

"Oh, that would make it that much better."

Kiley stood up and punched at him playfully. Dave quickly closed the distance between her previous location and the horse playing humans. This time she jumped on Josh and nipped at him.

"Hey, what up?!" he told Dave, surprised.

Dave woofed. They both tried to shush her. She jumped on Josh again, knocking him onto the couch. He tried to pull Kiley down too, but she jumped out of the way.

They kept laughing, which made it hard to calm Dave down. Somehow they managed to not wake up the baby during all their shenanigans.

"So, we good?" Josh asked Kiley, as she sat on the floor. Josh still lay on the couch, with Dave now looking all too comfortable laying across his chest, her tongue lolling out of her panting mouth.

"You and me? Ya," she replied, knowing what he meant but neither of them wanting to voice it.

"God, I'm tired," Josh said, rubbing his eyes. "I think it's time for bed."

Kiley was a little disappointed that Josh headed off to bed so soon. Dave was too. But if they did more than sit on the couch all day, they might be tired too.

22

On Saturday night, a bunch of the Tuckers went out to the Broken Wheel to have a few drinks. There was a live band playing. The parking lot was a sea of pickup trucks. Kiley supposed only someone who had been gone for seven years would notice such a thing. Since Kiley never made it out of the house, she decided to dress up tonight. And not in the clothes her mother would have approved of for a musical. Clothes that screamed Kiley to the core.

Being the only bar in town, it was needless to say that the Broken Wheel was very popular with the over 21 crowd. But Kiley had been too young to come here with her friends before her family moved away. The interior of the Broken Wheel was all dark wood. Kiley was pretty sure that the walls were made of barn siding. The open room was filled with wooden chairs and tables. Sometimes people got up and danced, like tonight, under the ceiling of exposed rafters.

Donna was at home watching the baby, so they had a different waitress tonight. Kiley, Wade and Jane, Josh, and Pete and Mackenzie were all there. The music was loud and it was hard to be heard over it. Kiley didn't have much to add to the conversation anyway, but she enjoyed people watching. She wasn't much of a drinker, so she only had two beers all night.

Wade and Jane were the first to head home, to check on the baby. Kiley didn't know why. Donna would have called if anything was wrong. You would think they would want to be away from Ethan as long as they could. It seemed like it would be a nice break to not have to worry about feeding him or changing him for a few hours. It was like they rushed home because they missed him or something.

Pete and Mackenzie headed out next. They were going to go on Monday to see about getting pre-approved for a mortgage so they could begin house shopping, and they wanted to spend some time getting their paperwork together tomorrow. They had saved up more than enough for a decent down payment in this favorable buyer's market. They had stayed with Evan in the farmhouse longer than necessary, mostly because Wade and Jane's housing disaster had scared them and made them leery of what kind of surprise a house of theirs might end up with. But Kiley chalked their change of heart up to the screaming baby in the room above them.

That just left Josh and Kiley at the table. Josh changed seats so that they were next to each other, to better talk.

A hand was suddenly firmly on her shoulder.

"Kiley? Kiley Riley, is that you?" a guy, who looked to be her age, was all smiles as he questioned her. He had blond hair and a very ordinary face. He leaned close to her, so he could be heard above the music and other conversations. He chose to do this by putting his body between Kiley and Josh.

"Yup, that's me. I'm sorry, I don't—" She smiled back, because she felt bad that she didn't remember him.

"Billy. Billy Eastman. We used to always have art class together?"

"Oh, right! How have you been?" She didn't really care, but she had learned in her author advisement from the publisher to be nice to everyone now. Anyone could be a potential reader. Or a possible Internet troll. In other words, fake it.

"Oh, not as good as you. I hear you write books now."

"Well, just one so far."

"Have you actually read it?" Josh interrupted, leaning in front of Billy and closer to Kiley. She could see each individual piece of stubble where it emerged from his skin.

"Well, no. But my sister did. She didn't even realize you wrote it until she read the author bio at the end when she was all done."

"I'm glad she liked it."

"Actually, she liked that Twilight stuff better."

"Smooth move, Ex-Lax," Josh chimed in.

"Have you been saving that one since the 80s?" Kiley asked Josh.

"And what would you know about the 80s? It's not like you were even alive then," Josh shot back.

"I am a writer. I do research. It's called *Nick at Night*," Kiley retorted. They were taking up their usual bickering routine. Billy tried to force himself back into the conversation.

"Ah, I was wondering if you are going to be in town a while, maybe we could go out sometime," Billy asked hopefully.

"Oh, that would be great, but I can't. I have a boyfriend." This was one of those times that being with Ted was just more convenient than breaking up with Ted. It didn't matter to Kiley that she couldn't go out with this guy, because she didn't want to spend time with him anyway.

"Oh, OK. Well, it was good to see you." He had retreated from the table before he had finished his sentence.

"God, the nerve of some guys," Josh said to Kiley.

"He was nice. But not my type," she stated, taking a long swig to empty her bottle.

"So nice guys are NOT your type?"

"That's not what I meant," Kiley fought back. She turned the patented leather cuff on her wrist back to the position she liked best, with the star snap pointed down.

"What IS your type?" Josh asked, close enough to her ear that his breath made the hairs on the back of her neck stand up.

"I—I'm not telling you." And in truth, she didn't know. What she found attractive about Ted was that he was attracted to her; that had always been the appeal.

"Can I get you another beer?" the young waitress asked Josh. She had brown hair that swung in a ponytail behind her head. It was sort of hypnotizing. It was in perpetual motion.

"Nah, I'm good. You?" he asked Kiley.

"No, thanks."

"Hey, are you the girl who wrote the book?" the waitress asked.

Kiley rolled her eyes, so that Josh was the only one who could see. The beer had made her goofy. She looked up at the waitress.

"Yup, that's me."

"Great book. I loved that the billionaire's daughter gets it on with the poor guy. And he sounded so hot! I would get with him, too," the waitress said as she spun around to go to the next table.

Kiley laughed and shook her head. "People get out of my book what they want to get out of it."

"She was too dumb to realize that they didn't just 'get it on,' they fell in love," Josh said, looking at the table.

"You read my book?" Kiley was floored. He raised his head. She studied him to see if he was lying. His eyes were warm and molten, like hot molasses, giving no indication that he was. And that had been a mistake, because now she felt all melty.

"Ya, I read it. And you should know, you need to put a real guy in the next book. Not some handsome yahoo with a six pack on his abdomen. A real guy. Time to lower women's expectations for what is out in the real world," Josh finished, seriously.

"Josh Tucker, you are full of surprises." Kiley shook her head, trying to clear some of the alcohol haze out of her brain. Instead, her head bobbed on her neck loosely.

"I wanted to know what all the excitement was about. Do people come up to you all the time and say stupid shit like that?"

"Yes. I thought I could hide out here and no one would notice. But it seems to be worse around here, because everyone knows me, or knows of me."

"Fame's a bitch."

Kiley giggled. "I am so NOT famous."

"Oh, I think you are. You are just too modest to notice. That's why those publishers of yours want you to write another book again so quick. Otherwise they would just ignore you and not give a fuck."

"I already had to change my idea. I wasn't getting anywhere with the first one," Kiley admitted. She hoped she wasn't setting herself up for his taunting.

"That's too bad. You'll find something worth writing about."

Kiley studied him carefully. It had been an especially warm day, over eighty in April. It was hot in the bar with so many bodies. Kiley had busted out a summer outfit for the occasion, so she was pretty comfortable. But Josh looked especially hot. He had sweat collecting in the deep creases that resided on his forehead.

"Is it just me, or are you sweating more than usual?"

"I sweat when I drink."

"But you don't sweat when you sit on the couch and watch *Third Shift.*"

"Because I'm not drunk then. Is that what you thought all this time? That I was at the bar every night?"

"That was the conclusion I drew as a writer... Why are you like that at night, then?" Kiley tilted her head and looked into his eyes. She really looked. They were warm and welcoming tonight. Usually they seemed to have a wall behind them. The wrinkles on Josh's forehead ran parallel. His forehead, combined with his long face, reminded Kiley of one of those wrinkle dogs, a Shar-Pei. It made him suddenly seem very sweet and vulnerable. His brown hair, that he always styled to look unkept, was now truly messy, as he had run his hand through it several times in the last half hour and destroyed the gel that held the delicate balance.

"That's just me," Josh finally answered her in his gravelly voice. He had picked up on the intended meaning of her badly articulated question. "I wonder if my dad thinks I drink away my paychecks as well," he chuckled. He smiled, showing all his white teeth. Kiley's heart did some sort of weird flip in her chest. It scared her.

JOSH

"Oh, I should be heading back to the farm," Kiley told Josh. She got up quickly.

"I can give you a ride. It's no problem." Josh slid his low-backed wooden chair away from the table, mirroring her movements. He couldn't let her walk out of here alone. She would never make it to her car without another yokel trying to hit on her.

"No, my car is outside. Plus, you've had even more to drink than I have."

"I only had four beers. I could have that for breakfast."

"Is that why you are so obnoxious early in the morning?" Kiley turned around to face him as he followed her out the front door of the bar. The humidity was so high that to move through the air felt like swimming. The scent of approaching rain was all around them. The night sky was thick with clouds. A streak of lightning shot across the heavens.

"Ha-ha. Very funny. I am a teddy bear when I first wake up. You want to find out?" Josh growled out the words. He raised an eyebrow at her suggestively. He didn't know what Kiley thought, but after spending all night with her, watching and listening to her, he was dead serious. He was now so intoxicated by her that he didn't know how he would ever be able to let her out of his sight again.

"You know I have a boyfriend," Kiley said, exasperated. They could now talk without having to yell to be heard.

"A boyfriend who has never come to visit you in the six months you have been here."

"I have only been here for four months."

"Seems longer," Josh said. Kiley glared at him, then turned in response, marching her muscular legs across the parking lot. The combat boots with the low heels clomped along. He could tell they were heavy and she wasn't used to walking in them. She stumbled every now and then on the gravel. He would love to have those boots wrapped around his back. A roll of thunder made itself known above the music escaping from the bar.

She was wearing black cut-off shorts tonight. They went well with the green camouflage tank top she wore. Josh had taken every opportunity he could to look down it tonight.

"Seriously, what kind of guy is this? He didn't even come to visit you for Christmas or for New Year's…" Another rumble from the sky interrupted Josh's tirade. It beyond pissed him off that someone would treat Kiley that way. Although, she didn't seem that heartbroken by it. He didn't believe their bond was that strong. If he had had a few more minutes alone with her cell that day, he could have confirmed it. She deserved better. She was worthy of being treated like a princess. She merited the courtesy of a break up if someone ELSE was done with her.

"He was with his family. And now he has started his master's classes. He is very busy," Kiley bragged.

Josh was unimpressed. They had reached her car in the parking lot. This was his chance. He had to push her, keep going. A bolt of lightning streaked in the sky. 'Screw my goals,' he thought. If he didn't have Kiley, then none of the rest of it would ever mean anything. If he couldn't keep her in Oakley, then he didn't give a damn about saving the rest of it. It could turn into a ghost town, for all he cared, for his heart surely would.

"But, what is he doing for you?" his tone caring, not smart-assed; he was careful of that. He could see the spark in Kiley's eyes dull as he hit a nerve. "This town is your home, but I can tell you aren't completely happy here. You are doing a great job faking it, but you are not cut out to be a nanny. You talk about writing your next book. You keep carrying around that notebook of yours, and never writing anything in it." A gust of wind blew through the parking lot, kicking up dust. Kiley's short black hair blew into her face. He pushed it aside with his hand, trying to maintain eye contact with her.

"And what is YOUR solution to my problems?" Kiley turned to face him fully, her back against the side of her white sport-utility vehicle.

This was his chance. Thunder roared louder as the storm came upon them. Josh leaned over and kissed her. He started slow and gentle, but as her body seemed to respond positively to his advance, he wrapped his arms around her tiny frame. He put all that had worked up inside of him these past few months into that kiss.

23

KILEY

Holy crap! Where had this come from?

Josh was kissing her. And it wasn't weird like she thought it might be. It was hot! The energy between them felt like an electric charge, vibrating every cell in both their bodies in sync, pleasurably. It was as though they had harnessed the lightning bolts from above. Quarter-sized drops of rain began to fall at an angle, soaking their hair and clothes. Josh wrapped his big arms around her, shielding her from the downpour. It felt warm and safe and, oh, she wanted more of this. She wrapped her arms around him as well. He was pulling away—NO!

She pulled back to see Josh looking toward the bar. The other patrons heading for their cars were looking their way and laughing at witnessing their intimate moment. He turned and looked into her eyes. His eyes seemed to be on fire. She did not know what he was seeing in hers.

"THAT is what you are missing," Josh said.

"I didn't know THAT existed," Kiley replied honestly. Now and then, her mind had wandered to impure thoughts about Josh, but she didn't believe any of those feelings would ever be reciprocated.

Josh smiled. "Maybe we should move this INSIDE the car."

"Ya, maybe." Kiley moved from the driver's door to the back door and pulled it open. Then she turned to look at Josh like an unsure teenager. This was all happening very fast.

"Ladies first," he held his arm straight out, inviting her into her own car.

Kiley simultaneously gave a look around the parking lot and jumped into the backseat of the car. While this gesture made Josh give a small laugh, he also surveyed the parking lot to see who might be watching as he got in and closed the door behind him. They were two eligible-to-vote, drinking-age adults, but it still felt like what they were doing was forbidden.

Josh and Kiley looked at each other in the car and smiled. A small stream of illumination snuck in from the yard light at the edge of the parking lot. The occasional flash of lightning reflected off the rain droplets that clung to their skin. It seemed providential now that Kiley had parked at the far corner of the lot.

Josh reached out for her, their lips drawn to each other like two magnets. They embraced each other. Josh's large hands rubbed up and down Kiley's back. She felt small and vulnerable in his arms. Somehow this turned her on even more. It made her want to show Josh that she could be just as powerful as him, in the bedroom, if not in the real world outside this car with the steamed up windows. It was different than when Ted begged her to be on top. Thinking about it now, he just seemed like a whiny little puppy compared to Josh. Josh had begun sucking on the hollow of her neck, just under her ear. At the same time, he slid his hand under her bra and grabbed her breast. He grunted a little as he kissed her. That turned her on too. It was a relief to get caught up in the moment, not having to be self-conscious about things such as noises.

A fire burned deep inside Kiley. She had never felt this way before. Suddenly nothing mattered but having Josh, right here, right now. She clung to him as if he were oxygen for her soul. He seemed to have no problem with this, as his actions mirrored her own. As she reached to undo his jeans, she had a fleeting thought that this experience would definitely have to go into her next book.

He pulled off her tank, then her bra. He sucked on her right nipple, rubbing it gently between his teeth. Kiley writhed under him. He did the same with the left side. She let out a moan.

Kiley reached into his pants, and took hold of his manhood. She began to stroke it. Josh, supported above her by his elbows, began to move his hips in the same rhythm as her hand.

"Oh, no. I can't handle that right now," he groaned.

Their lips met again as his arms tangled in hers as he pulled off her shorts and underpants.

"We'll leave these on," he said, careful to not pull off her boots.

She felt very vulnerable for a moment, laying there naked with his strapping body against her. Then his fingers hit her swollen bud of pleasure and she no longer cared. She let out a little moan as he slipped two fingers inside her ready opening.

"Oh God. Fuck. You are so wet. Please say you want to do this. Right now." The words tumbled from Josh's mouth. His rough voice made it all sound like a dirty purr.

"Yes," Kiley breathed.

If he felt this good now, how much better could it get with him inside of her? She didn't want to wait to find out. He quickly slid off his jeans and boxers. They fell to a pile on the floor of the car, with all the rest of their clothes.

Kiley arched toward him as Josh slid easily into her. She could feel the division of the head and the shaft as he plunged deeper inside. And literally the act of him entering her made her orgasm. Something Ted had never been able to do for her all the times they were together. Waves of passion washed over her. She moved in rhythm with him as the hunger overtook them.

"Damn, girl," Josh growled, burying his face next to her throat. His hard as a rock cock continued to undulate inside her. Their perspiring chests met as he reached a hand around to grab her ass. Her legs were against his torso, still wearing the black combat boots.

"Oh God," she cried as another orgasm washed over her. His breath caught in his throat as he tried to resist the urge to climax. Little whimpers escaped her now as she knew he wouldn't be able to hold on much longer. She writhed under him. Placing his calloused hands on her hips, he steadied her while he tried to control his final thrusts. His arms gave out with his release, and he lowered himself next to her on the seat as gently as he could.

"Wow. You have just as much fire in you as I suspected," Josh said, wiping the sweat from his forehead and trying to catch his breath.

"You have been thinking about this?" Kiley said, shocked.

"Haven't you?"

"Well, no. Not this, exactly. That's part of what made it so shocking and powerful."

"Hey, this isn't my first rodeo."

"It felt like it was for me."

"Nice ride," Josh said slyly, pretending to look around at the interior of her car.

"We are going to have to do that again sometime." The two bottles of beer had burned out of her system during the vigorous activity. Kiley didn't know what made her brave now. Hormones, she supposed.

"How about now?" Josh calmly replied.

"Really?"

"I'm good to go, if you are."

Kiley kissed Josh and the dirty dance in the backseat started again. By the time they both rolled into the driveway, all the windows in the farmhouse were dark. Dave met them at the door. She wagged her tail and sniffed them suspiciously. Josh went into the kitchen, while Kiley went straight upstairs, with Dave following her.

There was an implicit agreement between them that this maneuver would somehow make it less obvious that they had come home at the same time. Also, less obvious that they had just had sex. With each other. Twice. It was unspoken between them that too many other people in this house might hold a stake in anything that happened between them.

Kiley's skin still tingled where Josh had touched it. She was too keyed up to sleep. She threw her laptop on the bed and wrenched it open. Tonight she had a story to write. And she was going to start with the sex scene.

24

When Kiley woke up, it was morning. Or actually, 1:30PM. So, it was afternoon. Damn. She had missed seeing Josh over breakfast. And possibly lunch. But wait. Maybe that was a good thing. Did she want to see him?

Kiley couldn't even answer that question. Her laptop was next to her on the bed, the screen still glowing. She rolled onto her side and hit "save" quickly. Thank God she had plugged it in last night, so the battery couldn't die and lose her work. A quick glance in the lower left corner of the screen told her she had typed up 30 double-spaced pages last night. A good start. No wonder she had slept so late. She must have been up most of the night typing. She couldn't remember if the sun was up before she fell asleep or not.

As she tried to sit up straight, her abdominal muscles protested. Kiley put a hand over her stomach. They were very sore, but in a good way. Remembering last night, a small smile crossed her lips before she could stop it.

Kiley went and took a shower. She gathered from the noises in the house that it was Donna's day off and she was watching Ethan. Kiley put on some comfy clothes and worked on her writing till dinnertime.

She cautiously approached the table, but noticed that Josh's spot was empty. This wasn't that abnormal. A few times a week he would be MIA. Everyone else chatted and grabbed for dishes, while as usual Kiley kept to herself. Not only did she not want to let slip any of the thoughts in her head, but she was also busy shoveling food into her mouth. She hadn't eaten in 24 hours and she was starving. Both her body and her mind were drained, needing nourishment to recharge.

She needed a writing break, so after dinner she watched TV in the living room. She stayed on the couch long past when everyone else was in bed. About an hour later than usual, Kiley heard the front door open and close. She heard a coat being hung up and keys being slipped on the rack. Josh rounded the corner into the living room. His expression was guarded.

"Hey... I didn't know if you would be up tonight."

"I am. I was about to send out a search party."

"Aw, I always find my way home." Josh stood there in silence, trying to gauge Kiley's feelings. She sat there, doing the same.

"Look, I really don't know how you want to play this. I had a good time, but if you wanted it to be a one-time thing, I mean, that works for me." His voice began shaky, but became more confident as he came to the end of his statement. He rubbed his hand on the back of his neck, like it was sore. Kiley knew a thing or two about sore.

She shook her head in the affirmative, although she had no idea what she meant by that.

"Did I help with your writer's block?" he asked.

"Yes. Thank you." Kiley smiled.

"Hey, no problem. Glad I could help." Josh smiled back.

"Guess I'll be heading to bed," Josh said.

"OK. Goodnight," Kiley replied.

"Goodnight."

Kiley sat staring blankly at the TV for a few minutes. Then she had no choice but to go upstairs and work on her novel. Dave followed.

25

In the morning, Kiley was awakened by Jane knocking on her door.

"Sorry to wake you. Donna is at work today and I've gotta be in the office until one. Can you watch Ethan, or should I take him with me?"

"Oh, no problem. Will he be OK while I take a shower?" Kiley replied.

"I'll wait and take off when you are out," Jane concluded.

"OK. I'll just be a few minutes."

"Thanks," Jane said.

"It is the least I could do."

After Jane had gone, Kiley unfolded a quilt onto the floor in the nursery. She laid Ethan on his tummy and spread some toys around him. She read him parts of her story out loud. He gurgled every now and then in response. Next she carried him downstairs to the kitchen to get a bottle. He sucked it right down. She burped him, and then walked him around in preparation for his nap. She laid him down in his crib. Ethan started to cry, but that was the usual way his nap started. She backed out of the room and pulled the door until there was only a crack still open.

"That's a nice story."

Kiley spun around, startled by Josh's sudden appearance behind her.

"Th-thanks." It was a reflex reaction.

"But I think some of those parts are too racy to be reading to a three month old," Josh continued.

"How did you hear it?" Kiley felt a red blush spreading across her cheeks in embarrassment. She hadn't expected him, or anyone, to come home early for lunch.

"Baby monitor," Josh replied, smiling. As usual, it drew Kiley's attention to the stubble on his upper lip and below his bottom lip.

"Fuck," she blurted out, squinting her eyes shut at her own stupidity.

"Ya, you should just be glad I was the only one in the kitchen to hear. Or someone might have figured out who the 'scruffy, ruggedly handsome' hero of your story really is."

"And how do you know he is the hero?" Kiley made a snotty face at him, while not denying the character was strongly based off of Josh. She had just been in the kitchen, but Josh must have hid when he heard them coming.

"Oh, I can tell a description of a hero when I hear it." The smile was still on his face. "You know, you have a great imagination," he continued.

"But my story is still lacking something." Kiley let her voice drop just a little at the end.

"Maybe it's something I could help you with." They walked slowly towards each other in the upstairs hallway. Kiley felt like she was watching a scene in a movie. When they reached each other, she put her arms on Josh's arms. He put his arms around her back, pulling them closer together.

The last time it had been dark. They had been spontaneous and slightly inebriated. But how would this play out in the light of day?

Kiley's doubts melted as Josh's lips met hers. It didn't take long for him to deepen the kiss. She felt Josh's hand enclose around her right breast. Instead of protesting, Kiley ran her hands through his curly brown hair. Josh put his hands under her butt and lifted, placing her legs around his waist. She could feel the bulge in his jeans that was waiting for her.

How had Kiley ever written about love and lust and romance when she had never experienced any of it before Josh? There were so many things he made her feel that she did not even have the words to describe. But, well, maybe another go 'round would fix that.

He pushed open the door to his bedroom, and shut it behind them, leaving Dave in the hallway. She collapsed onto the floor against the door noisily, sighing in protest.

Josh backed up until he was able to sit down on the bed. Clothes had been left scattered all about the room, but Kiley didn't have much time to dwell on the living habits of the animal in front of her. She was still in his lap, still exploring his lips, his neck with her mouth. He pulled her black T-shirt off over her head. Josh stared admiringly at her breasts. His fingers traced around the edges of her black bra, then caressed each of them. She ran her hands up his arms. His muscles bulged as he massaged her chest and sucked on her neck. Kiley knew he was not the type to hit the gym, so it must be all the farm work that made him toned. She wanted to see more. It had been dark in the car the other night.

Kiley grabbed the bottom of his blue T-shirt and pulled it over his head. It mussed up his gelled curls. As she had suspected, he was well-built. His chest was robust and solid. He wouldn't be a centerfold anytime soon, but he definitely wasn't going anywhere if hit by a stiff wind.

"Well, someone is sure in a hurry today." Josh flashed an evil smile.

"I guess you must have done something right the other night." Kiley tried to flash a mischievous smile back at him. It must have worked, because he kissed her again like he might devour her. His tongue explored her mouth, and hers his. His perpetual stubble rubbed against her face. It was rough, but Kiley liked it. She suddenly wanted to know what it would feel like against other sensitive parts of her body.

Kiley was tired of waiting for him to take her bra off. She was ready to feel the skin of his chest against hers. She reached around and unhooked it herself. Josh groaned at the sight of her mounds of flesh, each no bigger than an orange, his hips bucking a little against her heat. He discarded it expertly over his shoulder.

Kiley took this opportunity to run her hands over his chest. Dark hair was scattered across his pecs. A tattoo was on the left side of his chest, a sun. The hair led down to places she could not wait to explore. She felt his abdomen, then ran her hands around to his back. This pushed their bare skin together. He plundered her mouth urgently. Josh's body was thick, but solid. The muscles might not be defined, like a billboard underwear model, but it was very sexy. She found herself rocking against the hardest muscle of all.

"Oh, fuck. You got to stop that or I'll never make it inside," he groaned into her ear.

Just the thought of him stretching and filling her again made her moan. They rolled around on the bed, trying to get each other's pants off. Josh leaned over her and reached for something from his dresser: a condom packet.

Kiley didn't know what this was between them. It seemed to be just stolen moments of sex. Maybe this was the last time they would be together like this. Surely Josh would get tired of her quickly. If she wanted something bad enough, she had to speak up and ask now, or she may never get the opportunity again.

"Wait."

"What's wrong? I mean, I thought...," Josh stumbled over his words, confused. They WERE both lying naked on his bed. He held the small foil packet in both his hands, about to tear it open.

"Yes. God, yes," Kiley began. She rubbed her hand against the hair on his chin. She could no longer resist touching it. "But first, I wanted to know what this would feel like..." Her fawn eyes raised from his chin to his meet his own eyes, and he smiled in understanding.

"Oh, shit. Ya." He grabbed her ankles and pulled her around, so that her head was on his pillow. He did it so quickly Kiley was afraid she might have fabric burn on her ass. He pushed her legs apart with his hands, running them up the inside of her thighs. Her body shook in anticipation. He ran a finger across her hot sex, dipping inside. She caught sight of his impressive erection, and instantly got wetter. He ran his hand back again. This time his touch combined with her own slick juices made her buck.

"Ya, I like that," Josh growled. Then he dipped his head down. She had a sharp intake of breath. But instead of digging right in, he started at her belly button, and nibbled his way down. When he reached her pleasure center, she couldn't hold her hips down, so he did it with his big, warm hands.

"Damn, girl. You are so sweet."

Kiley cried out, over and over, as the orgasms washed over her. She wanted to remember this feeling, to be able to write about it later. But there were no words to describe it when the whole experience was mind-numbing. Just when she thought one was going to be more than she could bear, a new one piled on top of it. Josh's lips, tongue, stubble—it scratched at her seductively. It was all just too much for her to handle with any sort of control.

JOSH

Ethan began to cry across the hall.

"Oh no. Shit. Look at what you did," Josh laughed at her. Kiley tried to push some of her hair off of her sweaty forehead. "You are a bad girl."

No one made a move toward the door. Ethan was already beginning to settle down again across the hall.

"Let me show you," Kiley cooed. Josh sat up to slide the condom onto his engorged length. Then Kiley pushed him back onto the bed, and threw a long leg over either side of him.

He almost lost it right then. DAMN. He loved those long legs of hers. Now they were straddling him as she shrouded his throbbing member with her nether lips. And it was his own fault that she was now so hot and dripping wet. It consumed him. It was in his nature as a man to want to thrust into her, but her moves on him felt just as good. She rode him up and down, like a carousel. Kiley was so wet and tight. And the way she threw her head back and let her mouth hang open. God. He couldn't wait to see what that sweet little mouth could do. Josh's mind wondered how soon they could sneak this activity in again. He wanted Kiley. Bad.

All. The. Time.

Josh was snapped back to earth as her orgasms tightened around him. He didn't want to peak now. He wanted to enjoy her tight, sweet body longer. He never wanted to let her go. Her riding him was just so hot now that he couldn't resist plunging into her. As they began to move in unison, it was too much. He couldn't hold back any longer. Kiley let out another loud cry. He took it as a compliment. A moan of his own slipped out. He shook his head. They could never continue this in this house if they couldn't learn to be quieter.

26

KILEY

Kiley knew she only had a few minutes with Josh before the others would begin to come home and pile into the kitchen for lunch. But she was enjoying her afterglow, and didn't want to leave him. Her head rested on his chest. She listened as both their breathing and heart rates returned to normal. She could feel the thin layer of sweat on both their bodies. She hoped Josh had had as much fun as she did. But she wasn't dumb enough to ask. If he had not, the embarrassment would be paramount.

She began to trace the tattoo on his chest. She realized it was placed over his heart. It was a yellow sun, with wavy orange rays coming out from it. As she got up the nerve to ask him about it, he kissed the top of her head. It made the fire begin to grow between her legs again.

"I like your tattoo. What does it mean?"

"Just that I like to bake in the sun and enjoy a nice, cold beer." He gave her a full smile, his mouth turning up at the corners at that odd angle and showing all his white teeth lined up like a piano.

"I don't believe you." Kiley shook her head. "Everyone's tattoos have meaning."

"Just means I got drunk one night and stumbled into the tattoo shop." His smile was smaller now.

"Even then, it would mean something to you. You put it right on your chest, on your heart. A place of honor," Kiley hedged.

"Shit, Kiley. You don't miss anything, do you?" She noticed he had used her real name for only the second time ever. The first had been in the barn. He was quiet for a few minutes before he spoke again. "It's for my mom."

"Oh. I'm sorry to bring it up then, if it makes you sad."

"No. The tattoo reminds me of the good times. She was like the sun in this house, in my life. Once she was gone, well, I just got this dark hole in my heart. The tattoo doesn't brighten it up, but thinking about her does. Also, I'm her 'son.' Get it?" He chuckled at his own joke.

"So, I was right. You put a hell of a lot of thought into it."

"Wade went with me to the tattoo shop. He wanted to get one too, but he chickened out. Big baby."

"I should have known Wade would be in the story somewhere."

Kiley continued to trace the outline of the small tattoo with her index finger.

"It feels nice when you touch it," Josh cooed.

"Does it?"

"I wasn't talking about my tattoo." He smiled again. Kiley playfully punched him. "But, now the tables are turned. What is up with YOUR tattoos?"

Kiley turned her upper right arm, so that Josh could get a better view of it.

"Well, it's a typewriter key, like off an old, manual typewriter. It is a 'K' key, to sort of symbolize the name I use as an author, 'K. Riley.' When I look at it, it reminds me of all I have accomplished. I know it's dumb, but it makes me feel proud," she concluded.

"Really? Because I more feel like you are declaring your love for the Circle K convenience stores," Josh said, smiling.

"What?! No way. It is done in black ink, not red!"

"I thought maybe you worshiped those giant cups of coke. Or maybe those slow-warmed hot dogs. Mmm..." Josh rubbed his belly, like he had just eaten a dozen hot dogs.

Now Kiley was laughing too. She thought her tattoo was well-planned, but Josh had made her think otherwise.

"And what about the other one?" Josh asked.

"Other one?" Kiley tried to play dumb, mostly just to annoy him.

"The other tattoo that I have already glimpsed several times on your left ankle."

"Ya, well. That is just Jack Skellington from *The Nightmare Before Christmas.*"

"Is it your favorite movie?"

"No. Not really."

Josh shook his head. "Then why?"

"Because," Kiley began, smiling, "I was young and wanted to piss off my mom. The opportunity to get a tattoo arose suddenly when I went out with my friend and her older sister. The older sister pretended to be our mom. They were both really goth, and I wanted to be. It was a movie we had watched together, so I figured it was a safe image to get."

"So you regret it?"

"No. I am glad I got it. I just wish it was something that was a more enduring image in my life. It still represents my rebellion of that time. Maybe I am still trying to."

"Oh, my little rebel," Josh said. His lips met hers, and all she wanted to do was feel him moving inside of her again. But noises that bubbled up from downstairs proved that the others were home for lunch.

They both begrudgingly got up and got dressed. Josh went into the hallway first, as they had been in his bedroom. When he saw the coast was clear, he waved Kiley out. She went downstairs to the kitchen first. Josh came down a few minutes later. Kiley tried to avoid eye contact with him. If her eyes met his warm, chocolate brown ones, she would melt into a puddle on the floor and the whole family would be witness to it.

27

JOSH

That night when Josh got home, he found Kiley furiously typing on her laptop in the living room. She was so involved, she hadn't even heard him come in. 'Maybe she is so involved she forgot to go upstairs and avoid you,' the voice of doubt in his brain told him. Once could have been a fluke, stupidity, anything. But two separate days of passion had to count for something. God, she was so cute sitting there with her pen in her mouth. She was using a computer. What did she need the pen for anyway?

"Oh, hey. Hi," she said, noticing him noticing her.

"Hi. What's new?" he asked casually.

"I sent my editor the first few chapters. She totally flipped. But now I feel even more pressure to make the rest of it just as good."

"Well, I guess 'congrats' and 'that sucks.' " He smiled at her. Kiley smiled back. He loved her one crooked tooth. It made her seem real and not like just some fantasy. He wanted to take her right here and now. He wanted her buck naked on that couch and screaming his name. Begging him to—

But they couldn't. Someone might see them (or hear them). Without knowing where this was headed, it was better if the rest of the family stayed in the dark.

"So, I overheard the juicy parts. What else is in your book?"

"Well, it's the story of a girl growing up with an identical sister..."

"Ahhh, writing what you know."

"That's what you THINK it's about. When the girl gets to be 18, she goes on a new experimental drug and her sister disappears. Her family tells her the twin was only a delusion." Kiley sat her laptop next to her and began talking with her hands.

"OK, starting to lose me here—"

"Then the ruggedly handsome guy gets involved, and it's possible it is all a government cover-up because they may have killed the twin sister," Kiley summarized, excitedly.

"That sounds... Well, actually, kind of awesome."

"Thanks. I was hoping you would like it." They smiled at each other. Josh leaned over and gave her a few quick kisses. He remained standing.

"I have been wondering something for months. I can't hold it in any longer. I have to ask: how can you stay up so late and get up so early?"

"I just don't require that much sleep, I guess. Plus, I have bigger things going on. I do like it that you wait up for me at night though. Too bad I never get to make breakfast for you."

"So, if you aren't at the bar till midnight every night, then I'm curious. Where ARE you?"

"Well, see that is Top Secret." He crossed his arms over his broad chest, as if he was holding in the information to keep it from escaping. "Besides, don't you know that curiosity killed the cat?"

"Don't tell me you have other conquests that keep you busy this late..." She gave him a half smile, which showed off that tooth again.

"Sure. I got bitches all over town," Josh said, staring down at her.

"C'mon! Tell me!" Kiley insisted, bouncing up and down on the couch.

"If I tell you, then I will have to kill you," he deadpanned.

"Oh, come on! I thought we were more than just friends now. You can tell me. I won't tell anyone."

"We were friends? When?" Josh asked, a goofy, confused look crossing his face.

"You know what I mean," Kiley said, exasperated.

Josh now took a place next to Kiley on the couch, and they kissed for several minutes.

"Talk," she finally said.

"OK. But I am taking a big chance, like, a huge chance telling you. No one else but me knows."

"No one knows where you are until midnight every night? How can that be? It's a small town," Kiley interrupted.

"No, everyone knows I work the 5:00PM-midnight shift at the Qwik Serv. Apparently everyone but you," he said, leaning over and bumping his right arm into her left arm lovingly. "But only you will know why I am saving up the money."

"Oh, so that is when you find the time to have a second job. But why?"

Josh watched a hundred different, possibly illegal, scenarios being imagined by Kiley flash within her eyes.

"I am going to build a golf resort," he announced.

"You are? But I didn't even know you liked golf."

"I don't. But I don't need to. I only have to see how it would benefit the area."

"Hey, is that what you were talking about in the office that day? Something about a business revitalizing the area?" Kiley hesitated.

"Yes! I didn't know if you would remember," he said, smiling wider at her. "I almost told you the whole plan that day. But I was afraid you would laugh it off as a joke. But, well, now you've seen me naked and you haven't laughed, so I guess I can trust you with this," he reasoned. He was so excited to finally have someone to share his vision with.

"Oh, I wouldn't laugh at that. Well, unless you were covered in bean dip or something," Kiley joked. She cozied up closer to him on the couch and ran her hand up underneath Josh's T-shirt.

"That could be arranged," Josh smiled as he kissed her.

"So, is there more to this idea?"

"Just that Alabama already has a huge tourism golf industry. All those folks up in Minnesota and Michigan and Ohio, they can't golf in the winter, so they come down here and golf for a week or two to get their fix. So, you need the golf course, hotel, fine dining, shops to occupy the wives if they come. I know it's a big idea, but so were home computers at one time. Now my friend Bobby builds custom set-ups in his garage."

"Wow. Do you think you can really do it?"

"I hope so. I'll have to find investors, but first I had to save up enough money so that they would know I was serious."

"Why not tell your dad? I'm sure he would help you out."

"No, see, that's the thing. He wouldn't." Josh shook his head and continued, "You heard him in the barn the other day. He doesn't see me as a 31-year-old adult. He still sees me as that 15-year-old kid getting arrested for setting the school on fire."

"You did do that."

"Yes, but I've changed. People change." Josh's voice sounded raspier than usual as it was weighed down with emotion.

"You do lead people to believe they can't expect much from you. I wouldn't suspect you had anything like this planned if you hadn't told me," Kiley said.

It hurt him to hear her, of all people, say what he already knew in his heart. He wanted Kiley to believe that he hung the moon. But he wasn't mad at her. She didn't say it to be mean, but to play devil's advocate. Josh's biggest worry all along, more than securing land or money, was how his checkered past could affect his future ambitions. He wanted to explain it to her, but he wasn't even sure that he knew himself.

"Ya, I guess it just makes it easier if no one expects anything out of you..."

"Except when you want to build a golf course," Kiley pointed out.

"A golf RESORT," Josh corrected her. He continued, "After I have investors lined up, I will need my dad to sell me a parcel of land on the edge of town cheap. He has more than he needs anyway, from everything he bought up from the other farmers who desperately needed the money. He paid them a fair price, of course," Josh added, as if he felt it necessary to defend his father.

"Do you need a business plan for all this?" Kiley asked.

"Yes. I have certain details worked out. I just need to type it up so it is pretty and makes sense to someone other than myself. I was kind of hoping I could find a girl in town with a computer to help me out."

"Oh really?" Kiley raised an eyebrow at him questioningly.

"Ya. I was going to see if I could maybe exchange services with her," he said suggestively.

"A trade? What do you have to offer?"

"Anything she wants."

And they kissed again.

28

Josh leaned on the hideous bright orange counter at the Qwik Serv. The finish had eroded right off the severely worn counter next to the cash register, from decades of abuse and wear. There was no way to quantify the amount of products, hands, and money that had passed over that very spot. The buzz of the fluorescent lights was louder than the country song currently playing on the radio. The song faded in and out, which was normal considering the broken antenna had only been repaired with Scotch tape. The cash register hummed, the fan blowing its hot air out across Josh's hands. He didn't notice. The latest book he had bought about real estate development lay behind the register, unread. That is what he used to do to make the time pass faster during the lull in customers. But now, he found himself glancing at the clock every few minutes, willing the hands to move faster. He had somewhere he needed to be, and someone he needed to see.

"Wake up, Sleeping Beauty. There is a customer that needs service."

Somehow Wade had come into the store, picked up coke, candy, and ice cream, then walked up to the register without Josh even noticing.

"I don't believe that I get paid enough to service you," Josh shot back with innuendo, slowly standing up to his full height. Unfortunately, he was still two inches shorter than Wade.

"Then I will assume everything is free tonight?" Wade said. Josh begrudgingly started to scan his items.

"Looks like somebody has a sweet tooth."

"Ya, Jane does. I will never understand chicks and their chocolate... But that's not something you have to worry about, as you don't have any chicks lining up for you right now."

Wade knew just how to make Josh's blood boil. If only he could tell Wade how wrong he was. Josh hit a few more buttons. Wade scanned his debit card.

"At least I didn't get attached to a ball and chain right at the prime of my dating years," Josh retorted back. It wasn't a good argument though. Jane was actually pretty nice, and let Wade get away with still having a little fun.

"Unless, of course, there IS someone, and that is what you were daydreaming about."

Shit. His asshole brother knew him too well. Josh chose to ignore Wade, as he bagged the items for him.

"I have never seen you thinking that hard about anything. You better be careful. Don't want you to strain your brain. It isn't used to that kind of activity," Wade smiled.

"Fuck off. Any girl I got is my business."

"Ah, so you ADMIT there IS a girl."

"I didn't say that."

"But you didn't not say that."

"If I did have a girl, I sure wouldn't bring her around you knuckleheads," Josh grumbled, hoping the discussion was over.

"Well, just make sure she likes you for the right reasons," Wade said. It was well-known that the Tuckers had the only money to be found in the town. Everyone else's prosperity relied on Tucker Farms continuing to run. It was also known that some meddling mothers would like nothing more than to marry off a willing daughter to a Tucker. Where there had once been five single Tucker men in town, including father Evan, now there was only Josh. Not that that increased the offers that he received much. Wade continued, "You haven't been out with as many women as I have. Your bullshit radar might not as good as it could be."

"It is detecting a lot of it right now," Josh replied. He scowled at Wade, making the wrinkles on his forehead appear more prominent. Wade just laughed as he headed out the door.

Josh took this as a slight. What, Wade didn't think he was good-looking enough to get a girl who didn't have ulterior motives?

Wade was throwing back advice that Josh had given to him seven years ago. Whether Wade realized this or not, Josh couldn't be sure. Advice Josh had dispensed unnecessarily, as it turned out. Jane had been just out of high school when her and Wade got real serious real fast. Josh had wondered if she was just looking for a payday. But months of moping on both their parts during their break up seemed to prove their love was legit.

Still, it bothered Josh that Wade could read him so easily. Was Josh walking around with "in love" written on his forehead? A big, goofy smile? He didn't think so. Maybe inviting Kiley to go with them up the water tower had been too obvious. But with all his waking thoughts (and his bed) being filled with Kiley, he knew it must be reflecting in his day to day routine. How soon till his other brothers questioned him? Or, God forbid, his father?

Josh himself didn't even know what was going on between him and Kiley. He didn't know if it was headed anywhere. He couldn't answer other people's questions when he couldn't even answer his own. He looked up at the clock again. One more hour before he could head home. He sure hoped that she was waiting up for him again tonight. If not for answers, then for her sweet lips.

29

Kiley headed to Fredrickstown, Georgia, home of her alma mater, Alva University. Also home of her supposed boyfriend, Ted. They had never had a lovey-dovey relationship. Now Kiley could not even remember if she had ever had strong feelings for Ted. She may not be able to name the feelings she had for Josh, but she knew they were stronger than anything else she had ever felt in her life. And the intensity gave her a strange high. The control it had over her was exciting. Every mile she put between her and Josh made her feel a deep longing. She felt it in her heart, and in her loins.

Breaking up with Ted had been a long time coming. Kiley felt she owed Ted a face-to-face explanation. Plus, he still had a few of her possessions that she wanted back.

First she went to the address she had for him on the fifth floor. It was no good. He had moved to a different apartment in the same building. The new tenant was nice enough to provide the correct number to her. She headed down to the third floor.

As she approached the door, she thought about how it was good she hadn't tried to send Ted a gift or a break-up letter. Having moved, he never would have received it anyway.

She knocked. She could hear laughing through the door. Ted opened it. He was only wearing boxer shorts. He had money in his hand. A girl with black hair who looked to be no more than a freshman was behind him walking around the room. She was wearing a T-shirt on top, and only her pink thong on the bottom. Her mocha legs were on display for the world to see.

The expression on Ted's face said it all. His mouth hung open in shock. His eyes were two orbs of surprise, magnified by his glasses. Kiley and Ted stood there in silence, staring at each other. He was busted, and he knew it.

"What's wrong? You need more money for the pizza?" the girl shouted, wondering what the delay was.

Kiley continued to stare at him, daring Ted to make a move or a sound. He finally gave in.

"It's not the pizza," he told her.

"Oh, hey." She approached the door. There was no shame or embarrassment in her lack of attire. "I don't think we've met. I'm Tiffahnie."

"Tiffahnie? The one you needed an autographed book for?" Tiffahnie had spoken to Kiley, but all of Kiley's words were directed at Ted.

"Well, ya. But that was before we were going out," he replied.

"So you used one of my books to pick up a new chick? Gee, thanks. I am glad I could help you get laid."

"What's going on?" Tiffahnie asked.

"I came to break up with you, Ted. The long distance thing isn't working. I came to tell you I have been seeing someone else, which obviously you have too. No biggie," she said. No reaction crossed Ted's face at this statement. He wasn't surprised that Kiley had taken a lover. He wasn't sad. He wasn't anything. A pain bolted through her, prickly and burning, at that realization. "But at least I had the decency to drive up here to end it with you. You were just going to leave me hanging. And I can't believe you would move in with someone else without even breaking up with me first?"

"You didn't break up with her? You told me it was over months ago," Tiffahnie looked confused.

"If it was over months ago, why would I still be calling you and emailing you and sending free books? And I want my stuff back!" Kiley demanded.

"What stuff?" Ted asked, stupidly.

"My CDs. My sweatshirt. The box of stuff I left with you when I went on tour."

"Fine. Just a sec." Ted went into another room, presumably to gather her stuff.

"I'm sorry. I, like, totally didn't know. I thought he took care of all this while I was off at nationals."

"Nationals?"

"I'm a gymnast."

"She's an Olympic hopeful," Ted bragged, walking up behind them. He handed Kiley a cardboard box.

"It's my last chance," she said humbly. It was loaded with parental pressure and self-doubt. This girl didn't know what she was in for. She deserved better than Ted.

"I'm glad I came here today. I not only got my stuff back, but my self-respect as well. Enjoy your life of being a hanger-on of the famous. It suits you, Ted."

With that, Kiley turned and left. She passed the pizza delivery guy on the stairs. She couldn't wait to get back into her car and head to Oakley. She was so over all this. Her whole relationship with Ted had just been a lie. Ted's true motives were now clear.

She stormed out the door of the building. She wrenched her car door open so hard she almost fell to the ground. Instead, she used that momentum to swing herself back, leaping into the car. She was upset, so the only thing she could do was cry. This made Kiley pissed at herself, but all that did was made her cry more. She viciously jammed the key into the ignition, and twisted it. The engine sprang to life. Kiley was about to slam the shift knob into reverse, but grabbed her cell phone instead.

Before she left, she texted Ted the picture she had taken of Josh's water tower masterpiece. A smile tugged at the corner of her mouth, just for a second.

Kiley had to think that her upbringing, which lacked an obvious outpouring of love, must have had something to do with her latching on to the first guy that showed any interested in her, even though he wasn't good for her. She continued to intermittently shed tears. After all, she was human. She had been dating him for two years. While she had never had any delusions that they would get married someday, she had thought it was a real relationship, not just a lie. It had given her a confidence boost to think that someone was capable of loving her.

She remembered that she used to challenge things that made her feel uncomfortable. Whether it was a teacher who gave her a grade she disagreed with on a research paper or an editorial in the university newspaper about how they weren't doing enough to promote recycling on campus, Kiley used to stand up for things she believed in. An introvert at heart, she could still scrap with the best of 'em if it meant sticking up for something she was passionate about.

And with Ted, well, she had let him convince her that his ideas were better than hers. She always caved in when he challenged her. And she couldn't put her finger on why. He had really done nothing to earn her respect in the time they had gone out. It must have been simply the fear of losing him. Ted had been the first guy to show long-term interest in Kiley. She had been afraid that no one else ever would. Well, Josh seemed to now. But what if Kiley had become one of those women who always needed a man in her life to make her feel whole? She didn't want to be that person. Whatever she was becoming in this time out in the real world, she wasn't sure that she liked it.

And what about Josh? He was waiting for her back in Oakley. Kiley loved being with him. She loved talking to him. He was great to spend time with while she was home, but that's all it was. They didn't have a future together. Josh was not the marrying kind. He would always be a bachelor. He cooked for himself. He didn't mind his own mess. Josh was self-sufficient. He didn't need a wife.

Kiley would enjoy her thing with Josh while it lasted. But she wouldn't kid herself about what it was. She had to protect her heart. She wouldn't let herself get hurt again.

Kiley began to cry harder. She didn't know why.

JOSH

Josh stroked Kiley's black hair as she laid next to him on his bed. It was getting longer. She hadn't gotten it cut or dyed since she had been home. Her roots were beginning to show an obvious lighter brown. He kissed the top of her head, and then kissed her lips. Her tongue explored the depths of his mouth. He held her face steady with his hand flat across her cheek and let her continue the kiss.

Josh didn't used to care about much of anything. For years he would work all day just to head to the bar at night, to have a beer and try to pick up the same chicks in town that were always there. He did enjoy playing pranks and causing trouble. He could admit to himself that he had wasted a lot of years without having any sort of direction. But he was ready to move on from that now. More and more every day, he wanted Kiley to be a part of that. But he was afraid that she wouldn't be able to see that he had changed. Or, was trying to.

Kiley had been different tonight. Her lovemaking had an urgency to it, like she had something to prove. Josh assumed her breakup with her boyfriend had not gone well, but he had not asked. He couldn't imagine anyone stupid enough to lose Kiley. That sure was not Josh's plan. Just her being hundreds of miles away from him for the day had strained his heart. The more he had thought about it, the more he had realized that he couldn't begin to imagine living without her now. Her body, her smile, her verbal sparring. But he wasn't sure tonight was the right time to bring all that up with her.

This was the first night they had taken the chance of being together in the house, in his room, while everyone else was home. It was now 2:00AM. They tried to be quiet. It was hard to gauge how successful they had been. After all, he found it hard to come and listen at the same time.

They always had relations in his bedroom. He had a queen size bed, while Kiley only had a twin. Plus, her room was like Grand Central Station. Donna was always bringing her food or Jane was asking for babysitting or Mackenzie was asking for fashion advice. Everyone knew to leave Josh the fuck alone when he was in his.

Her pale skin was a contrast to his, tanned dark in the daily sun. It looked like milk. He wondered if he bit her if it would taste like it as well, rich and nurturing.

"Can I ask you something personal?" she asked, looking into his eyes. He never wanted to look into another set of eyes. Ever.

"Sure." There was a difference between them tonight as well. Whether they were getting closer or growing apart, he could not determine.

"I've been wondering for a long time, why are you so competitive with Wade?" Kiley asked.

"Oh. You noticed that?" Josh replied.

"Hard to miss," Kiley smiled at him.

"It should be obvious."

"Why?"

"I mean, Wade, looks like a fuckin' movie star. Gets all the girls. Wouldn't any brother be jealous of that?" Josh summarized.

"Randy and Pete don't seem to be."

"It's complicated." Josh grabbed the TV remote off of the bedside table, but he made no move to turn it on. He rotated the controller over and over in his hands. A large, wooden entertainment center that had seen better days sat at the foot of his bed. It held a HDTV way more massive than was necessary for the square footage of his average-sized bedroom. Below it on the shelves were every video game system that had come out in the past decade. Controllers, game cases, and wires were stuffed in here and there into any extra inch of space.

"So?" Kiley tried to break into his thoughts. She succeeded.

"See, Wade and I are less than a year apart. When we were little, my mom used to actually dress us alike, until we started school. Wade and I are both outgoing. But somehow, when he does it, everyone finds it charming. When I speak my mind, everyone thinks I'm a dick."

"You are two different people, you know?"

"I know. But we came from the same family. How different could we be? Somehow, he got all the looks in the family. Then chicks like you go and write books about guys with six pack abs, like Wade's got. Don't get me wrong, I got a six pack too. It is in my fridge, that's all."

"Well, maybe my new book can change that."

"People will know you wrote about me when it comes out."

"We have over a year before it will go on sale."

"Maybe we should tell everyone sooner, rather than later," Josh began.

"You want to let everyone know we—" It was obvious by her reaction that Kiley had not expected this.

"Well, we could spare them all the details. We could call it 'dating.' We could even start going on real dates, if you wanted." He knew that he wanted to.

Kiley was quiet. She closed her eyes before she answered.

"We don't have to sneak around like kids. We are both adults," he hedged.

"I know... I am not ready yet, OK?" Kiley answered softly.

"OK." Josh paused. He was worried he might regret it, but he had to ask. "What happened with the boyfriend tonight? Ted, is it?"

Kiley chuckled before she answered.

"Your water tower graffiti spoke the truth. Ted is so boring that he made me forget that I used to be feisty," she answered.

If their night on the water tower hadn't been such a nice experience to share with her, he would have regretted taking her up there with him. It carved a pretty big chink in his plan to show everyone, including her, that he was more responsible now.

She rolled over and hugged Josh, laying her head on his chest. Sometime after he fell asleep, Kiley snuck back to her own room.

The next morning, Josh actually slept late and missed breakfast.

30

Josh knocked on Kiley's door, then slowly opened it. She was sitting at the little desk against the wall, typing on her laptop at lightning speed. He entered the room, closing the door behind him. He hoped the rest of the family would take the hint and give them some privacy.

"Hey. I thought you would be working at the store tonight," she said, surprised.

"I took the night off," Josh began. He wanted to tell her he had taken the night off specifically for this task. He wanted to tell her that his stomach had been in a knot all day about asking her for her assistance. Not being able to eat, he had taken a drive in the country instead of coming home for dinner. He had parked at the edge of town and stared out across the field of burgeoning vegetation. He envisioned the buildings and greens and fairways that could possibly one day replace the crops on the edge of Oakley. Anxiety had gripped his heart then, and the mirage had all vanished. But he had seen it. For that minute, his dream had been real. It was the universe's way of pushing him forward.

Approaching Kiley for this task was the next phase in his grand master plan. The plan for this life, the salvation of the whole town...maybe one day the blueprint for Kiley's life as well.

"Sorry to interrupt you. I know you are working on your book or whatever...," he hesitated at the foot of her bed.

"Actually, I am working on my blog."

"Your what?"

"You don't know what a blog is? It can be like an online diary, or a business tool. It is a website where you dispense tidbits of useful or interesting information one week or one day at a time."

"For who?"

"For your followers. Whoever happens to find you using a web search or a social media share. For me, it is the fans of my book. I can keep them updated on any appearances and my next book. My publisher sort of made me. You know, you should get one of these started to help attract investors for your golf project."

"Funny you should say that. That is sort of why I am here." He handed a folder full of loose papers and a spiral notebook like students use to Kiley.

"What's all this? Did you write a book?"

"No. That's my business plan. Or, well, what needs to be in it, anyway. All my research and notes."

Kiley thumbed through the scraps of paperwork.

"How long have you been working on this?"

"The idea came to me about five years ago. It is only in the last two or three years that I have actually been collecting notes and stuff," Josh paused. "How old were you when you first realized you wanted to be a writer?"

"I was sixteen. Of course, back then, most of my time was taken up with bad poetry. It really helped me survive adolescence though."

"Well, some of us are not lucky enough to know what we want to do with our lives as a teenager. Sometimes it takes longer than that to figure it out."

Kiley smiled at him. Josh returned it, knowing the uneasiness was showing on his face.

"I don't mind helping, but I have to guess that writing a business plan is very different than writing a novel. I mean, I only took one class on professional and technical writing in college, and I have forgotten all of that. I don't know the structure or how to format it..." Kiley shook her head, looking overwhelmed. Maybe she was just picking up on how he was feeling. He soldiered on, trying to sound brave and knowledgeable.

"Well, that first page lists a few websites that are supposed to help with that. I was hoping—well, praying—that you could help me use those outlines and then make some fabulous version with everything I need to include."

"Dang, boy. You must think I like you or something," Kiley replied with attitude.

"I was hoping..."

"Hoping what?"

"That you like me. And would help me." Josh smiled that wide grin at her. He was trying to be charming. He was trying to push down the feelings of vomit again. He imagined it came out looking fake, like a used car salesman.

"I guess. I mean, I will. But we aren't going to get his done all in one night," Kiley answered tentatively.

"That's fine. But we need to get started tonight."

"Why the sudden rush? Haven't you been working on this for a while now?"

"Yes. But, well, this is the next step. And if I don't do it now, I might just chicken out and never go any further. I could take the money I saved and just use it to go on a drinking binge in Las Vegas or something."

"Oh, let's both do that!" Kiley replied a little too emphatically.

Josh raised an eyebrow at her questioningly.

"But I get what you mean. We will see how much we can knock out tonight."

"Thank you. Thank you sooo much." Josh sat on Kiley's lap at the desk. They kissed. The old wooden chair creaked under the burden of both their weights. They laughed.

"OK, OK. Back down. But, we will need snacks. Can you at least order us a pizza?" she begged.

While they were preoccupied, Dave jumped up on Kiley's bed. She scooted the quilt with her nose and paws into a nest, and then laid on top of the paperwork.

31

KILEY

It was annoying that Oakley had almost no stores. The grocery store and the hardware store were about it. If you wanted a new bed or television or a clothes washer, you had to make the trek to the nearest large town. Kiley had forgotten what a bother it could be to have to drive up to Huntington for anything else one might need. Huntington being two hours away, the people of Oakley usually waited until they had several errands to do before heading up, or until one task was so pressing it was no longer avoidable.

The drive to Huntington hadn't seemed like such a bother to Kiley today with Josh in her car beside her, although he did seem annoyed by the purpose of their trip. He continued to complain as they walked into the menswear store.

"I told you, I don't need a new suit. I showed you the one I keep in the back of my closet for church and funerals. It is still perfectly functional," Josh whined.

"That old thing?" Kiley replied. She began to look at the racks closest to the door. A salesman, who was with another customer, nodded an acknowledgement to them. She continued, "First, you didn't even have a bag over it, so it is all dusty. It is worn. Remember when you tried it on for me? It didn't fit you right, and I don't believe it is entirely in style any longer."

"Just needs a trip to the dry cleaner is all. It will be as good as new."

"I don't think so," Kiley laughed at him.

"Sorry for the wait. My name is Sean. How can I help you today?" the salesman asked, already looking Josh over to try and guess his measurements.

"Hi. This gentleman here...," she began. Josh snorted. "...Has a very important business meeting coming up. He needs to look his best."

"Nothing too fancy. Or too pricey," Josh said, waving his hand.

"We aren't afraid to pay for quality. He may be wearing it quite often," she clarified, glaring at Josh.

"Something contemporary and professional, but simple," Sean said, smiling. He led Josh over to a little platform in front of a three-way mirror. Josh stood on it, and Sean proceeded to get his measurements. He turned and started to walk away, but Josh grabbed him on the arm.

"Not anything too slick. I don't want anyone to call me one of those metrosexuals," he said, worriedly.

Sean chuckled. "I don't think we will have a problem with that." He headed into the backroom.

"You are really closer to being a lumbersexual," Kiley informed him.

"Then why aren't we shopping for chainsaws?" he frowned, then continued. "J.K., now he is going to pull out all the most expensive stuff."

"So? It will cost a little, but it is a necessary business expense. It is all about presentation."

"I thought that is what the business proposal was for."

"The facts of the proposal will get you in the door, but a nice suit will sell your plan as well as color copies ever can. It shows you are serious."

"I don't like the idea of having to dress up to talk to people. My ideas should speak for themselves."

"Trust me. I feel the same way you do. You see my holey jeans and stretched-out T-shirts every day."

"Ya, I do," he growled at her.

"But I have to dress up on occasion. This is a step to your future. Just imagine how great it will be when someday you and I can both sit around being our own bosses, more or less, in whatever we like... Or even nothing at all."

"Fine, fine. You win."

Nudity always wins.

"I can't believe I get to dress you up like a big Ken doll!" Kiley clapped her hands together excitedly.

"Hey, hey, now." Glancing at the back of the store, Josh saw no sign of Sean. "I think the salesman is gay."

"Good. He will help us make more fashionable choices then."

"Kiley, I didn't know you could be so stereotypical."

"After this, I can drag you off to get a haircut."

"What? What's wrong with my hair?" Josh asked, running his hands through his curly locks.

"I like it just fine. But it will help you look more polished." She stood on her toes and kissed his frown. "I just want you to succeed. You know that, right?"

"Yes. Thank you."

Just then, Sean emerged with several suits, motioning for Josh to head to the dressing room.

"But I am not enjoying any part of this."

"I know."

32

JOSH

The little bell on the door rang, but Josh couldn't hear it. He did spot the hottest woman he had ever seen walk through the front door of the Qwik Serv from his spot inside the cooler, where he was restocking the drinks and watching for customers through the glass doors. He quickly opened the metal cooler door, jogging through the office and out onto the sales floor of the store. The black night wore on outside beyond the windows and the door.

"Hey, J.K. I've been waiting for you. I thought you got lost on the way back from Huntington."

"I decided to make the most out of my drive and had dinner with the fam while I was up there."

"So, did you have time to pick up the copies? It was the main reason you went."

"Calm down. One business proposal. Hot off the presses!" Kiley boomed, pulling paperwork enclosed in a black folder from behind her back. "I even put the cover on, so you can see how it will look. The extras are in the car."

Josh grabbed the folder aggressively from her, as if he was a thirsty man and it was a canteen.

"Oh my God. This looks so professional. I couldn't have done it without you."

"No biggy. Just the magic of standardized formatting and the color laser printer at the office supply store," she boasted. "And your Dad can't accuse you of printing it on the copier in the farm office, because it won't have that black smudge that always comes out on everything. Does it look like how you wanted? Is all the information correct and in the right place?"

"Yes. I mean, this is based on our last revision, right?" Josh asked. Kiley shook her head in the affirmative. "I feel a lot better about it since you had people look it over and add input. I have never done this before. But now I feel like I have a little more confidence that this makes sense and could actually be persuasive," Josh finished. He stared at the proposal as if it was something mythical, as if it was leprechaun poop that could disappear in an instant.

"So, are you really going to do it? You are actually going to talk to your dad tomorrow?"

"I think I am. I can't stand feeling this nervous knot in my stomach anymore. The anticipation is killing me. The worst he can do is say no, right? Put an end to all of my hopes and dreams."

"He won't say no."

"I don't know how you can be so sure." He shook his head doubtfully.

"Because it is a great plan, that's why. And it benefits the town. The hopes and dreams of everyone won't have to rest on your dad anymore... They will all rest on you!" Kiley said sweetly, smiling at him.

"You are NOT helping the knot in my stomach."

"If you are going to complete this massive undertaking, you are going to have to grow some balls, big man. Step one is to talk to your mean old Daddy."

"Yes. I know you are right," Josh paused. "Are you sure you won't go with me?"

"Uh-uh. No. Never. But I will be with you in spirit."

"Thanks again, for all your help."

"Anything for my LOVER!"

A regular customer came in right then, getting off his second shift job no doubt, interrupting their revelry.

"Get out of here. I've got work to do," Josh tried to sound gruff, but she could still hear the anxiety in his voice.

While the customer was perusing the beef jerky, Kiley leaned over the counter and gave Josh a quick peck on the lips.

"Wait up for me?" Josh pleaded.

"No doubt," she replied, and bounced out the door.

33

KILEY

Kiley had snuck back into her bedroom from Josh's room before everyone else got up. She hadn't wanted to visit his room last night. She tried to reason with him, that speaking with his father, he would need all the rest that he could get. He should be spending these last precious hours sleeping, not up late canoodling with Kiley. It would be best for him. But he was so keyed up that he had been bouncing on the balls of his feet when he came in the door from the store. The only logical way to burn all that energy off, he had informed her, was some love-making. It sounded like bull to her, but he fell into a peaceful slumber soon after. She had slept a few more hours in her room, until everyone was gone to work on the farm, including Josh. Then she woke up with a startling realization.

What should have arrived two weeks ago had not.

And she had no one to complain to but herself. If you don't use any birth control, you can't blame the condom company or the pill manufacturer. The first night, at the bar, her and Josh had used nothing but luck. It felt like Kiley's luck had run out. She had been on the pill when she was with Ted in college, but she had let her prescription run out while on the road.

When she had slept with Josh at the bar, it had been the last thing on her mind. It had seemed like the universe was pushing them together: the warm night, the thunderstorm. It had seemed like they were meant to be. Kiley had fooled herself into believing nothing bad or inconvenient could have come out of that experience.

It appeared that she was wrong.

What was she going to do? She couldn't go buy a pregnancy test at the grocery store. The town rumor mill would have her as knocked up before she ever had a chance to pee on the stick. Normally, under these circumstances in Oakley, one went to the convenience store. Sure, they were known for their confidentiality to the rest of the town, but surely they gossiped between employees. One of which was Josh himself.

Josh.

How could she tell him? Should she?

34

JOSH

Josh had made a formal appointment to meet with his father in the farm office this morning. When he had told his dad he wished to see him at such a specific time and location two days ago, it was evident on his father's face what he suspected. He was positive that Josh was going to all out quit, or at least give notice. This had made Josh smile at the time. Now it made him even more nervous. His father's mind was already made up about what this meeting was regarding. How would that influence his reaction to Josh's business proposal? Maybe he would just go ahead and fire Josh, get it over with, and three years of work and planning wouldn't matter anyway.

Josh parked his pickup truck outside the farm office. He climbed out and shut the door, careful not to rub his new black suit against the dirt that perpetually clung to the side of the blue Ford F150. He had bought the suit just last week. With what he had paid for it, he couldn't afford a trip to the dry cleaner anytime soon.

Kiley had also convinced him to get a haircut. It was his same style, just more trimmed. He no longer had curls at the base of his neck, making him look unkept. God, Kiley. She had done so much for him in just the month she had known about his dream. It was as if she had arrived at just the right time. She was everything that he needed. He wouldn't let himself think of her as an "angel", but he couldn't think of a better word either.

Josh walked into the office, and Jane gave him a look of surprise, but said nothing. This made Josh feel uncomfortable as well. He didn't know what to say to her. His father's office door was open and he had an appointment, so he just walked in, pulling the door closed behind him. Seeing Jane just made him think of Kiley again. At that moment, Josh knew that no matter what went down now with his father, he had to have a talk with Kiley about their relationship soon. Maybe even today. He needed her by his side.

His father looked up and smiled at Josh's appearance.

"April Fools' Day was last month. You are a little late there, son."

Josh kept his composure. In the end, this is pretty much what he had expected coming in. He pushed on.

"I'm here with a business proposal for you," Josh began, handing his father a black folder, and keeping one for himself.

His father didn't look at the paperwork in his hand. He finally took his eyes off of Josh's suit and met his stare.

"Is this a joke?" he laughed.

"No, it is not, sir. You have always had the prosperity of this town in your best interests. I bring to you today a plan that will be in line with your own goals." Kiley and Josh had agreed on using the respectful generic noun of "sir", as "Dad" and "Mr. Tucker" didn't really fit this particular set of circumstances.

"You said you wanted a meeting with me," his father started, shaking his head. "I expected you to finally grow a backbone. I thought you were quitting. Or moving out. Or both. Are you telling me that is not your plan?"

"No, sir. My plan is in your hands. It has been thoroughly researched. I have done due diligence up to this point. Before I can proceed and find investors..."

"So you want my money? That's what this is about?" His dad shook the unopened folder at Josh.

"No sir, quite the opposite. I would like to draw up a legal agreement for a parcel of your land of roughly 800 acres with the understanding that when I find interested investors, you will sell it for the agreed upon sum," he paused, taking a breath. Josh couldn't blame his dad for not believing all this. Josh was having trouble believing these words were coming out of his own mouth. But it was what he had rehearsed with Kiley.

Oh, push her out of your mind. For now.

"You want my land?" His father continued to shake his head.

"No, sir. I want to purchase your land and rezone it."

"800?"

"Give or take, sure. 800 acres would allow enough land to be secured to provide luxury housing surrounding the three courses. Such real estate is very desirable. It would be another revenue stream."

"This is what you have been working two jobs for?" He pointed at the folder.

"Yes, sir."

"You really think you can pull this off?"

"I can't tell the future, but I would love the opportunity to try. But that all depends on your willingness to part with the land. As we are all aware, there is no land in Oakley or surrounding areas that large held by a single owner, other than yourself. This is a good plan. I could implement it anywhere, but I would love the opportunity to bring wealth and prosperity back to Oakley." Josh was starting to actually feel the words he was saying. It must have shown to his father.

"Who are you, and what have you done with my son?" His father was still smiling, like this was all still some type of joke. Josh had put so much time and effort, not to mention heart and guts, into this project. His nervousness was passing, and anger was trying hard to replace it. He knew this would be difficult to get passed, but he could do it.

"In this venture, I would rather you not think of me as your son. We are simply business associates. And once the land deal is done, you won't have to interact with me on this any further than as fellow Oakley business owners."

"So, you've really thought this through?"

"Yes, sir."

"Huh. Well, this is quite the surprise. Of course, I can't give you any answers right now. I have to review this, and have my lawyer review it, possibly the town council...," he mused, finally opening up the folder and looking inside. "Golf, eh? I never learned, but I have heard there is money to be made there."

"There is. It could revitalize the entire town. Bring in people to work at the resort. Those people would need to build houses to live in town. They would need more stores and gas stations, entertainment. You are very welcome to present it to your lawyer. But Mr. Drexel has already reviewed the particulars, and he would just need the specifics to begin the paperwork. Mr. Ross and Mr. Clark, who sit on the council, have reviewed it as well. They were very excited by it, which I have no doubt you will be too once you have time to review it."

"Well, I guess that is what I will have to do then... You got any of these so-called investors lined up yet?"

"No, sir. That is the next phase."

"You don't know this, but I have been looking for a good investment."

"With all due respect, sir, I believe our professional lives would be best served by being linked as little as possible."

"Well," his father laughed, "Maybe you are right about that. Come back in next week and we'll talk about this more, alright?"

"That sounds very fair. Thank you."

Josh turned and practically ran out of the office and out to his truck. He didn't even notice that Jane was no longer at her desk. He hopped in, not paying any attention to his suit. He beat his fists against the steering wheel like a drummer, throwing his head back against the seat. It helped to release all his pent up emotions.

This was happening!

He instantly started sweating, and pulled off his suit jacket as he started the car. He wanted to go find Kiley and tell her all that had happened. Josh wanted her to be clear on what part she would play in his future as well.

35

KILEY

Oh, God. Josh and his big dreams. He was supposed to be talking to his dad about the plan this morning. Actually, right at this instant.

Kiley didn't want to be the cause of him giving up on saving the whole town. Choosing her over 3,000 others would be tragic. But that could be easy enough to remedy. She could leave Oakley anytime. Announce her visit was over, go anywhere in the U.S., finish her book...

And drag a secret baby on a book tour? C'mon Kiley, pull it together.

Or maybe she could swear her sisters and mother to secrecy. She could still have a support system. But that would still involve never returning to Oakley. Or Josh would find out. Josh would know. If Josh knew, he would have to do the right thing. He would want to marry her, support their child. All great things, if they would not derail all his other plans.

Kiley would leave Oakley and never come back. She could.

Except, there was one thing keeping her in Oakley that she wasn't ready to leave yet...

Josh.

It was action time. She quickly stripped out of her pajamas and threw on some clothes. She didn't pay attention to if they were clean or not. She would jump in the car and drive to Huntington. It was a big city. There were tons of stores there where she might purchase a test. She just had to manage to avoid three people: Miley, her mother, and her aunt. With a quick search on the social location app, she would be able to pinpoint Miley. The other two would be harder. Kiley would just have to hope she had a little luck left after all.

It turned out that she did not. In the kitchen, coming home for lunch, she ran right into Jane. Except she seemed to be home sooner than usual.

"Hey, sis. Where are you off to in such a hurry?" Jane accused, or so it seemed to Kiley.

"I just thought I would run up to Huntington, do some quick shopping." Kiley tried to regulate her voice and her breathing so they sounded normal. She failed.

"Are you alright? You seem a little—"

Bloated. Nauseous. Glowing?

"Manic."

It was just as accurate as the words Kiley had thought of.

"Sure, I'm great. Just need to get out of this house."

"You want some company?"

Fuck. How to play this one.

"Nah, I'm good. I mean, you have to get back to work." Kiley could see the shift in Jane's eyes. She had overplayed her hand.

"Actually, it is really slow today. I was thinking about taking the afternoon off anyway. Donna has the baby. Oh, and I didn't tell you the best news! Wade and I found out we can move into our house in a few weeks! So, I could totally use a chance to shop for the necessities—curtains, wastebaskets, furniture. Everything! C'mon. Let's go. Girls' day."

The wheels in Kiley's head worked overtime at a frenetic pace. Two things occurred to Kiley simultaneously.

One, she wasn't going to get out of taking Jane with her. She would have to find a way to sneak off and make her purchase unnoticed.

Two, she was free to leave. No strings. With Jane and Wade moving into their own house, they would resume the normalcy their life should have had when they bought the place, if it had been livable. There would be no further reason for Kiley to stay with the Tuckers. Or in Oakley. The decision was made. Past knowing that she was definitely going to leave, she made no further decisions yet.

Although there WERE other decisions to make. Kiley had always considered herself pro-choice. She had read the book *The Cider House Rules*. Anyone who had read that book became very familiar with—The Process. But this was HER. Her own decision. She still totally believed that everyone should have the option if they decided to take it. But now that it was personal, well, it seemed off the table. Especially now that Kiley had spent so much time with Ethan. A baby was not just some abstract idea anymore.

And, well, it was part Josh. She lov—liked Josh very much. She didn't want to hurt something that he had been a part of creating. Kiley pushed that particular issue to the back of her mind and refused to let it surface again. She couldn't even begin to see through the tears that were welling up in her eyes.

"Hey, do you happen to know what is going on with Josh today?"

"What? Why? What do you mean?"

"He made an 'appointment' to talk to his dad today, which is weird enough. Then he came in dressed in a suit. It is really odd behavior for him. Usually he just comes in, does the minimum, and heads back home again. I don't know what to make of it."

"Oh, ya, I have no idea. Did you, uh, see him leave the office?" Kiley asked.

"No, I left to come over here and ask you if you knew anything. Seemed to be a private conversation anyway, behind closed doors."

She was trying to find out what Josh's father had said. That could have an affect on her decision. But, would it really? Kiley could tell when Jane had questioned her, she had given away that she knew damn well what Josh was up to. Now Jane was even more suspicious of her behavior. Kiley knew today would be a huge day for Josh when she had gone to bed last night, knew it could alter his life and dreams. She had assumed everything would hinge on the decisions of his father. She just didn't realize her decisions would be such a large part of that equation.

"We should get going," Kiley mumbled. She threw on her jacket and wiped the excess moisture from her eyes in one smooth motion. Kiley walked super-fast to her vehicle, trying to create a strong enough breeze to dry the rest of the tears in her eyes. She was in the car, had the door shut, and the car started before Jane had even opened the passenger door. Kiley knew she looked extra suspicious now, but she didn't care.

36

In order to buy all the things Jane needed, they had to make an unscheduled stop at her house. It was an unassuming little house, right next to the schools. Kiley could not even imagine all the times she had walked past it heading home after cheerleading practice, and not even given it a second glance. Now it was her sister's house, where she and her husband would raise their family. It is where Kiley would come back to visit. How would it be feasible for her to come visit Oakley and possibly never see Josh again? Any plan that Kiley tried to formulate kept crumbling like ashes from a fire. The same way her nerves crumbled more every minute.

Jane unlocked the door and flipped the light switch. Although there was already plenty of sunlight flooding in the windows, obstructed by nothing but the stickers that showed that they were new and energy-saving, the lights popped on.

"Oh my God! There is power! And light!" Jane jumped up and down like she used to when—well, never.

If this was almost done, what had this place looked like before the contractors had started? It looked like it was being rebuilt after a bomb had gone off. The walls were white. But there were streaks and spots over them of an even whiter white. It reminded her of a kid with zits trying unsuccessfully to cover them up.

"I'm sorry that I am so excited about having power, but there hasn't been any here since they ripped out all the old wiring. Oh, and I have walls!" Jane threw herself against the wall as if it was a long-lost lover. When she backed away, she brushed fine white dust off the front of her gray hoodie.

"These walls don't look done," she frowned. Jane's giddiness had distracted her from watching Kiley too closely. Kiley was glad for that.

"Oh, there weren't walls here at all last week. This is the living room. The drywall is completed in here. Once we put on a coat of primer and a few coats of paint, it will look just fine. I may have to draft you to help paint."

Ugh. Kiley thought paint involved fumes. How could she avoid that activity without being obvious why?

Jane pranced around into the other rooms. Kiley wandered into the kitchen. She braced herself against the counter with her arms extended, bearing all her weight upon them. Her back arched in an unnatural way, as if she could crumple at any second. She looked down into the gaping hole in the countertop that would someday be the kitchen sink. Kiley felt like puking into it, then pushed her eyes closed tightly. She wished she could just go to sleep and then wake up from this bad dream.

Kiley's mind was still swirling around at a mile a minute. But some random panicked thoughts were sticking more than others. The baby was part Josh, so she wouldn't be able to let herself part with it. She would have to raise it on her own. But could she do that? It was taking a whole houseful to tend to little Ethan. If it was just Kiley vs. a baby, all on her own, the baby might win. If she stayed away from Oakley, there would be no help for her. No one to watch the baby for a night out or relieve her for a nap or a shower. Her breath sped up as this vision of her future reached her heart and lungs.

"Spill it."

Damn it! Jane had snuck up from behind. Well, she probably didn't have to sneak, with Kiley being so preoccupied.

"It's nothing. I'm just happy you are getting your house back," Kiley lied. She didn't make eye contact with Jane and couldn't even muster a smile.

"Kiley, tell me," Jane urged.

"I might be pregnant."

"What!... I'm sorry. It's just, I haven't even seen you with anyone while you were here. Or was it Ted!"

"No, it wasn't Ted." Jane had never commented on Ted one way or the other to Kiley. But even she must have sensed it wasn't the relationship that her little sister deserved. If only Kiley could have seen that herself.

"Have you taken a test yet?"

"No. That's why I was going to Huntington. To buy one."

"You could just pick one up here in town at the Qwik Serv."

"No, I can't," Kiley replied slowly.

"Why not?"

"Because HE will find out," Kiley conceded.

"Oh my God, Josh! When?" Jane concluded.

"A month ago. However long it takes to be knocked up."

"Just once?" Jane asked.

"Just one night that we didn't use something." Kiley and Josh had been "together" twice that night, but that was more information than Jane needed at this juncture.

"Kiley, you've got to tell him," Jane pleaded.

"We don't even know if there is anything to tell yet," she replied, holding out a small shred of hope.

"We need to find out."

"This isn't the plan I envisioned for my life," Kiley whined.

"I know." Jane pulled Kiley into a hug. They embracing until they heard the storm door handle pushed, then the squeak of the inside door opening.

"Oh, that must be Bob," Jane said. "He is the latest contractor; the one actually getting the job done." The wooden door blocked their view of the new visitor.

"Hello? Kiley?" a scratchy voice called.

"Shit, it's Josh," Kiley whispered.

"I can tell you have been hanging out with him. You are using the same vocabulary."

"Maybe I can hide," Kiley whispered. But just then Josh looked around the door and spotted them standing in the kitchen. The room was wide open, but a counter separated the space between them. Kiley was glad for that. She didn't think she could handle any physical contact with Josh at this moment. She would definitely lose it.

"Oh, hey Jane. What are you guys up to in here?"

"How did you know we were here?" Kiley asked, staring at the floor.

"I saw your car out front."

Of course. Duh. That was nice and logical.

"Well, since Wade and I can move in soon, I wanted to start buying some furnishings." Jane threw herself into the role, but she wasn't a very talented actress. Josh seemed to know that something was up.

"We were going to head up to Huntington." Kiley didn't know if that was still the plan, but she had to say something.

"Hey, that sounds like fun. Maybe I could tagalong." Josh still stood in what was going to be the living room, talking to them over the kitchen counter. Kiley wondered if this would eventually be a pass-through, like everyone had become so accustomed to at the Tuckers' farm house.

"No! I mean, it will be all shopping and boring, girlie stuff," Jane tried, but this charade was too far gone.

"Exactly," Kiley tried to agree with Jane, but somehow the word came out very short and with a slight British accent, a bad one at that.

"Wha—what's going on here? Are you guys planning a surprise birthday party for me?"

"Is his birthday close?" Kiley asked Jane, not even trying to lower her voice.

"No. Three more months," Jane replied.

All three of them stood there in silence.

"Kiley, what is going on that you are not telling me?" Josh asked. She could feel his eyes boring into her. It was hard to resist making contact, especially when he used her name, but she continued to look at the floor. His gaze must have shifted to Jane.

"I think I'll leave you two alone for a minute to talk. I'll be waiting in the car."

Kiley looked up to watch Jane almost run out the door. Nice. If Josh wasn't spooked before, he was now.

"What is going on, Kiley? Tell me," Josh urged.

Kiley knew that there was no way she could tell him the truth, but she had to tell him something. This was going to be painful sooner or later. She might as well get it over with now.

"Look, Josh, I really like you...," she began, the words awkward and broken.

"What's going on here? Is this like a practical joke or something? Are you recording this on your phone?" Josh asked, a nervous laugh escaping and echoing into the empty space.

"I just don't think we are compatible..."

"Why does it sound like you are just making all this up on the spot?"

Because she was.

"I think it is better if we end things now, rather than later."

"You are breaking up with me? Why? This makes no sense..."

"We will both save ourselves a lot of pain later if we just end it now."

"Pain? Why would there be pain? Kiley, you are talking at me, not to me..."

He put his hand under her chin and raised it up so that he could look into her eyes. She saw that he was still wearing his suit, although the tie and jacket were gone. His shirt was unbuttoned at the neck, ultra-white as only new shirts can be. Her body ached for more of his touch, no matter how subtle.

Kiley almost gave in to him, almost surrendered herself over to him.

And her heart broke into a million pieces right then. She hadn't realized it, but before this morning's revelation she had begun to imagine a future with him. One where they went out on dates and sat in front of the fire on a cold night, with Dave curled up on their laps. A future where maybe someday her last name would be the same as Jane's again.

Her chest ached. She was trying to turn her heart to ice all morning, to protect herself while she put distance between everything she wanted to hold close. Now being under his powerful stare, the edges were trying to thaw. She was doing all this to protect Josh. Couldn't he see that? Why wouldn't he just let her go?

Josh put his hands on her upper arms, trying to hold her in place. It failed. Kiley wrenched out of his grip and ran towards the door.

"I—I'm leaving town. It's over," Kiley yelled behind her as she opened the door and ran out into the midday sun. She hoped that he had not heard the tears in her voice that had threatened to betray her.

"Don't you feel better now that you told him?" Jane said, as Kiley jumped into the car.

"Sure," she lied.

"What did he say?"

"I—I didn't give him a chance to say anything."

"Do you think that's wise?"

"I think I missed wise a few weeks back," Kiley said, slamming the car into reverse down the driveway, trying to avoid Josh's truck parked on the street. It occurred to Kiley that she had not even had a chance to ask Josh about how the appointment with his father had gone. Now she felt like the lowest of low. She had either made a good day bad, or a horrible day worse.

They drove to the Qwik Serv. Jane and Kiley decided that it would be the least suspicious if Jane went in to make the purchase. She was married. It wouldn't seem that odd if her and Wade had another baby so soon. Although Jane was eternally grateful that she was not. One infant was enough for her at a time.

A quick call by Jane proved that Donna was still visiting her sister with Ethan. They headed back to the farm house. Luck was on their side. There was no one home.

"Why couldn't we just take it at your house?" Kiley asked Jane.

"Because there is no toilet yet. Why do you think WE are not living there!" Jane answered, irritated.

37

JOSH

What the fuck had all that been about?

It was like being shot. Her announcing her departure, it hurt like hell.

Josh was thoroughly confused as he pulled the door of Jane and Wade's house shut behind him. He left it unlocked, as he had no idea what else to do with it. It was not like Jane had left him any instructions before she disappeared with his girlfriend.

Wait.

Where had that thought come from? He hadn't ever thought of Kiley as that before.

Sure, things seemed to have been going great between them lately. There was all the outstanding sex. And they genuinely seemed to like each other. Or, at least he had thought so before today. She had been so much help with the business stuff. He hadn't even gotten to tell her about the meeting with his dad. Maybe she felt he had used her for her writing and organizing skills. Maybe it was too similar to how that despicable piece of crap Ted had used her.

Josh climbed into his pickup truck. He sat there for a minute, staring at the dust coating on his windshield. The sun shone off it at just the right angle where he couldn't see through it at all. He was suddenly blind to his future. He couldn't even see the road three feet in front of him.

He had done something to scare her off and he had absolutely no idea why. He was juggling between being hurt and being pissed off.

"Fuck!" he yelled, slamming the palm of his right hand against the steering wheel in anger. It was a violent hit, much harder than the joyful thumps he had given it just a few minutes ago when leaving the meeting with his father.

He began to slowly rub the sore spot on his right hand with his left.

Pissed off won. Fuck her. Kiley had seemingly fallen into his life, she could just go and fall back from where she came from.

Unfortunately, when he pulled into his driveway, it was behind Kiley's little white RAV4.

He really didn't want to see her anymore right now. But he was very curious why they had told him they were going to

Huntington when they had not. Maybe she decided not to waste another second in Oakley and had begun to pack. Screw it. He was hungry. It had been an exceptional morning and he had worked up quite the appetite. Plus, he wanted to get out of this monkey suit.

Josh came in the entryway and there stood Kiley and Jane, looking like two deer caught in the headlights.

"Did you know he was coming?" Jane asked.

"No," Kiley replied.

"For people sneaking around, you are failing miserably," he tried to say without a smile. But even though they had fought, her trying to break his heart, Kiley still had that effect on him.

"You didn't tell him, did you?" Jane said.

"There is nothing to discuss," Kiley pushed.

"Tell him, Kiley," Jane urged. Kiley's mouth fell open.

"There is nothing to tell," Kiley growled back.

"Kiley might be pregnant."

"Jane!" Kiley reprimanded.

"He should know," Jane said.

"Wow, that's the first time I have heard you sound like actual siblings...," he paused, watching Kiley seethe with anger at her sister. "Jane, can you maybe excuse us for a couple minutes?" Josh tried to diffuse the situation to his advantage. He needed to talk to Kiley alone.

"Sure. I'll be upstairs," Jane shuffled out.

"So, you think—?"

"I don't know yet. I'm late."

"And the first time, we didn't—"

"Ya."

"And is there any chance—"

"No. Just you."

"And this is why you, uh, broke up with me?"

"I am not out to get anything from you. You don't owe me anything."

"I have never thought that you were... This will be OK, Kiley. Either way. We can come out and tell everyone and no more sneaking around."

"I'm leaving."

The pregnancy thing hadn't phased him. Maybe it hadn't sunk in. Maybe, he hoped it would be the anchor to make her stay. But her stubbornly sticking to her earlier resolution when he now knew the reason behind it made him ill.

"You're what?" God! Why was he making her say it again!

"Jane and Wade are moving into their house with the baby. And it's time for me to move on."

"But I don't want you to."

"I can't get in the way of your dream. It means too much for the town."

"Screw that! Is that why you are insisting on leaving? I couldn't care less about that stupid golf course, compared to you—to a baby!"

"There is no reason for me to stay any longer," she repeated her same argument again.

"Me! Stay for me," he pleaded.

"Look, I've become very fond of you. But it is all just lust." Kiley's eyes met his. They were the color of a dry northern dirt road, and just as lonely.

"You can't even recognize love when it's in your arms, in your bed," Josh shot back.

"It's not love." Tears filled Kiley's eyes.

"Maybe not for you, but it is for me," Josh whispered back. She was lying to him and he knew it. He just didn't know how to break through this wall of denial to reach her common sense.

Kiley had no comment. Josh gathered her in his arms and hugged her. There was no way he was letting her go. He had never been very good at oral persuasion; today seemed to be the day he had to improve. Now was the time to make it count.

"Why don't you want people to know about us?" he asked. It was the question at the heart of all of this.

"Because, if people know, then this is real. If our relationship is never real, then it can't end badly. I can't be hurt."

"So this has to do with that asshole Ted?"

"No, it has to do with me. That I couldn't see that he was just using me. He is a fame whore."

"That was you and him. This is about you and me."

Kiley just zoned out. She showed no emotion at all. He tried to make eye contact, but Kiley wasn't home. She was a zombie. Josh tried a new tactic.

"I love you, Kiley. I want to be with you forever." Wow. He had said it. And ten minutes ago he had blanched at using the word "girlfriend." But he meant it.

"You are just saying that because I could be carrying your child."

"I want us to be together forever. That offer stands, either way."

"But I don't want to force you into anything," Kiley said. Her eyes met his, tears streaming down her cheeks like rivers. He had finally broken through her resolve. The walls had come down.

"It isn't forcing me if I am standing here in front of the door, begging you not to leave," Josh said.

"You really want me to stay?"

"Yes. I thought I made that clear. I have been crazy about you since the first day you walked through that door."

"Really?"

"You couldn't tell?"

"I just assumed you were like that with all women."

"Only you, K. Only you. Now, let's go see if you are good at taking tests."

38

KILEY

Jane crept back down the stairs when the raised voices subsided. It was apparent that she wanted a minute alone with Kiley. Josh left them to go up and change his clothes.

"Kiley, I have never told you this, but you are so strong," Jane started.

"What? No. It is just an act," Kiley replied, holding the two unopened pregnancy test boxes in her hands.

"No. You have the strongest will out of all of us. You decided what you wanted to do at a young age, and now you have made that dream happen. You worked hard. You saw it come to fruition. You never gave up on yourself. And now is not the time to start. Life hands us things that seem too big, like Mom and Dad's divorce. But somehow, we get through it."

"Where is all this coming from?"

"I have always thought so. I guess I just never put it into words and told you before."

"Ya, because our house was like that."

"I wish I was as strong as you. I am weak. I found that out at college," Jane stated.

"That's not true."

"I have to have others to lean on. You have never been like that, Kiley. I wish I was like you. You were always secure enough in yourself, even as a teenager. But maybe now is the time for you to learn that there are people you can lean on, if necessary," Jane paused, smiling at Kiley. "What is the worst that could happen? You have a baby with a good man you love, who loves you?"

"Ya," Kiley sniffed at her sister's outpouring of compliments. "I guess you are right. It just, well, isn't my plan."

"Plans can change. And that is especially hard for me, with my personality, to accept. But look at Wade and I. We have made the best of a bad housing situation. We pictured bringing our son home to our own cozy little house. That hasn't happened yet, but we brought him into this house overflowing with love instead," Jane finished.

Kiley nodded in acknowledgment. Josh joined them. She went into the half bathroom, off the entryway. Josh and Jane kept yelling at her through the door, making her nervous.

"I've got to concentrate here! A little quiet, please," Kiley shouted.

"Pee on them both at once, to save time," Josh yelled.

"Good idea." Then Kiley was curious. "Are you sure you haven't done this before?" she asked. She didn't know that much about his dating history. Maybe there were a string of Josh Jr.'s around town that she just didn't know about.

"No, I swear," came his reply. And she believed him.

Once Kiley had prepped the tests, there was nothing to do but wait. They all fidgeted and tried not to talk. The timer finally chimed on Jane's phone.

"It's time," Jane announced.

"I can't look," Kiley hid her face in the couch.

"I'll look," Josh said.

He got up and went into the bathroom. He came back out.

"Well, they are in agreement. You are not pregnant."

"What?" Kiley stood up on the couch to be taller than him. "Are you joking?" she grabbed the lapels on Josh's red flannel shirt that hung open over his gray wife beater. "If you are joking, I swear to God I will punch you! I swear to God!" she began shaking him.

"I'm not. Does that make you more relaxed?"

"Yes! Don't you feel better knowing I'm not?" she cried.

"I told you, it really didn't matter to me either way." Josh added, "Of course, I would much rather have a little control over major life events."

"Congrats, Kiley," Jane said. She touched her sister's shoulder and then left the two of them alone.

JOSH

"Thank you," Kiley said.

"For what?" Josh asked.

"For being there. For being you." Kiley kissed him.

"Now can we tell people? About us?" Josh begged.

"Jane already knows."

"I guess it depends," Josh said.

"On what?"

"On if you are still planning on leaving. I know you can take your career anywhere. But my future is tied to this town." At least with no baby in the picture, he would know if she was really choosing to stay for him.

"Tied to this town? So your dad said 'yes'?" Kiley asked excitedly.

"Well, first he laughed in my face, and then he said he needed a week to think it over. But I am counting that as a 'yes.'"

"I'm so happy for you," Kiley said, throwing her arms around Josh. "For us," she added. She was still standing on the couch, so his face was actually being pressed into her boobs. But it was an overall touching moment, so he decided now was not the time to make a dirty joke. "I'm sorry I didn't ask about your meeting earlier. I was being selfish and pre-occupied."

"It's fine, as long as you promise me that you will stay."

"Yes," she answered. He pushed her down onto the couch, and crawled on top of her. His mouth covered hers, needing reassurance of her decision.

When they stopped kissing and turned to the doorway, they realized that everyone else in the house, except Jane, had walked in the front door and was watching them make out. The audience's mouths hung open in shock, except for Wade and Donna, who looked like they had it all figured out, probably before Josh and Kiley had themselves.

"Hey everyone, Kiley and I are going out. Anybody got a problem with that?" Josh made his voice sound more gravely and deep. He tried to sound tough.

"You are just full of surprises today, son," his dad said as everyone quickly moved on into the kitchen. Kiley giggled and buried her face into Josh's shirt, still clinging to him.

"You sounded so mean."

"Did I scare you?"

"No, I liked it. A LOT…"

"I'll remember that," he paused. "Well, lunch table conversation should be interesting," Josh told her.

39

For the follow-up business meeting with his father, Josh decided to wear his new baby blue-button down shirt and a tie, but left the suit jacket at home. Kiley called it his red power tie. He didn't know how powerful he actually felt today, but at least this time both he and his dad knew what the score was walking into the meeting. There would be no misunderstanding that he was about to resign.

Jane smiled at Josh warmly as he came into the office. She motioned him on into his father's office. Kiley had told Jane about the plan. Everyone else was still in the dark at this point. Hopefully, that would all change very soon. Last night he and Kiley had stayed up late designing a huge sign to put in the field, announcing the new development coming soon. Kiley told him some mumbo-jumbo about it sending a positive message to the universe. It sounded like hooey to him, but he couldn't deny he needed all the help he could get.

"Hello, sir," Josh said, approaching the desk.

"On time two meetings in a row. If only you were that punctual to do your farm work," his father said, smiling. Josh sat in one of the pair of chairs in front of the old, battered metal desk.

"I want you to know how serious I am about this project." Josh let his father's comment go. It was just who his father was. And Josh needed this land deal, he really did.

His dad leaned back in his chair and smiled. Josh knew that this was a good sign.

"Tell me again why you are so passionate about this. At our last meeting, you made an appeal to my efforts for saving this town. But I have never seen any interest out of you for such things. Is this all about the money a project like this could generate? How do I know you really have the best interests of Oakley at heart?"

If this was the biggest thing plaguing his father's thoughts, that meant that he couldn't find any fault with the nuts and bolts of the proposal. Josh felt it was obvious he was doing this to benefit the town, but if he had to spell it out for the old man, he easily could. That was a minor hurdle compared to others his father may have asked him to jump.

"I have lived here all my life, the same as you have. I have no desire to live anywhere else. But despite your best efforts, Oakley continues to lose more businesses every year. I have heard visitors who come to town to see loved ones comment that our downtown looks more like a ghost town." His father cringed in his seat at hearing it stated so bluntly, but Josh continued. "I can sum up my desire for this project with your desk."

"My desk?"

"Yes. I remember, you bought that ratty old metal desk off the public school. Why were they having that sale again?"

"That was when they combined the middle and high schools into one building. Less upkeep on two buildings. Roof repairs, heating, all that," his dad stated.

"And that was both possible and necessary for the school system because there were so few students left in the Oakley school system. I remember that the village also hoped to make some revenue by selling the high school building. But it still sits empty, years later, now a dangerous eyesore."

"Are you going somewhere with this, or you just feel like reminiscing?"

"In Oakley post-resort, people will move nearby so that they can work there. It will need housekeepers, groundskeepers, waiters, cooks, administration. Their children will attend Oakley Public. We will need to not only fix the schools, but expand them. The tax money from these new residents will be the feed to grow them." Josh realized he sounded like he was talking about fattening up a cow rather than a school system, but his dad seemed to get the point, nonetheless.

He sat staring at his son across the top of the desk. The smile was gone, but the look in his eyes was replaced with something else. Josh had never seen his father look at him like that before. It was the look in his eyes when Randy got married, and when Wade hit the winning home run for the baseball state championships. His father was proud of him.

"Well, there really isn't any reason to beat around the bush. I had my people review it, and they all say it is sound. We can move ahead to the next step in this process. Come up with a proposal for the specific parcel of land you want. We can get it surveyed, and all that."

"Thank you so much, sir. I really believe in this." A smile escaped, but otherwise Josh was able to contain his excitement.

"I can tell that you do," he nodded his head. "You could have tried something small, like building a house, or even a store or an apartment building. But no, you have to build a whole damn resort. It's go big or go home for you I guess, eh?"

"I think you are finally starting to understand me."

40

It had been a very long drive, even though it was all interstate freeways. With the stop at the burger joint for lunch, it had been six hours. But it would be worth it. Sure, Josh was trying to turn over a new leaf, be a man of business and all. That didn't mean that every now and then he couldn't let some of his old/true self escape. He felt it necessary to stand up for his girlfriend, even if she would never say so to him. It was a good thing she was gone to visit her mother for most of the day. Maybe his absence could go undetected.

Josh parked his truck outside the unassuming apartment building. It made him sick to think that Kiley had walked out of this building, crying over that douchebag. He got out and slammed the door behind him. He popped his knuckles and laughed to himself. Sure, Josh had to snoop through Kiley's email to get the address. But she hadn't caught him this time, so he hadn't had to deal with her wrath.

He went inside, climbing up the stairs. He found the apartment number he was looking for and knocked on the door. Two tall guys who looked like they stepped right off the basketball court answered the door. They informed him the tenant Josh was searching for now lived downstairs. He climbed back down two flights of stairs. Tired of this runaround, he knocked on the door loudly. He hoped this guy wasn't too big, not that that would stop Josh from serving him a little justice. From the description Kiley had given, Josh wouldn't have much trouble. He heard a scuffle behind the door, and then it opened.

The tiniest little skinniest piece of shit Josh had ever seen stood in front of him. Total science geek. Actually nerdier than he had pictured from how Kiley had described him.

"Ted? Ted Bailey," Josh asked.

"Yes, that's me. But look, I am on my way out of town," Ted said, straightening his glasses. "I don't have time to buy magazines or whatever right now. So if you would excuse me..." He turned away, like Josh was actually going to let him close the door. Josh's foot was already blocking the door casing.

"Oh, no. I think this will only take a minute," Josh said, smiling his full evil smile at him. It conveyed the desired effect, because Ted moved back a step. Josh's eyes picked up on movement behind him further into the room. An African-American woman was gathering together bags and suitcases. She wore only a tank top and shorts, showing off her muscular arms and legs. Josh smiled and shook his head.

"What will only take a minute?" Ted asked dumbly.

Hmmm. How to proceed. Usually Josh didn't punch guys wearing glasses. He couldn't wait to pummel this guy, but he did have a conscience. Prescription glasses could be pricey.

As quick as lightning, Josh grabbed at Ted's face, pulling off his glasses and flinging them to the ground behind him onto the floor of the apartment. Like a total fight virgin, Ted looked behind him, following where his glasses had gone.

"What the—"

When he turned back around, there was a fist thrust right into Ted's nose, then another into his eye.

"Ahhh!" Ted screamed.

"What's going on!" the girl cried, running up to the door.

Josh gave him another punch in the stomach, doubling Ted over in pain.

"That was courtesy of Kiley."

The girl ran up to aid him. Ted looked up weakly at his attacker, but made no move to fight back.

Josh looked admiringly at the girl. He shook his head again.

"I will never understand how a worm like you ends up with such hot women," Josh said, then turned and walked down the hall, back to the stairs.

41

KILEY

Jane took Ethan to go visit their mother in Huntington. Kiley tagged along. Miley was supposed to be there too. Kiley couldn't help but think that if she had failed the pregnancy test (i.e. a positive result), this could be the last visit she would have with her family for a while. But, she had her life back. And she wanted to start living it more wisely.

Their mom lived in Huntington, in the house her sister Jamie had inherited. Their mother had moved there when she divorced their father, when Kiley and Miley were just starting their sophomore year in high school. Jane had just gone off to college. Even after all these years, their mother was still a bit of a mystery. Sure, she was responsible, polite, met all her obligations. She had worked full-time and managed to make it to all their afterschool activities. Her biggest flaw to the outside world was that she didn't make homemade cookies for the endless fundraising bake sales—she always picked up a box from the bakery.

But to them, she was just never that forthcoming with her feelings, especially love. To be fair, their father had been the same way. They didn't see much of him now that he had moved to Jackson. Kiley felt that maybe he was just a loner at heart.

They had taken Jane's car, because it was the one with the baby seat in it. Jane parked on the street out in front of the old Victorian house. Kiley tried to balance on the curb while Jane spent what seemed like an eternity unstrapping her now five-month-old baby. It was amazing how fast Ethan had grown. He seemed to be twice as big now as when he was born.

When they arrived, Miley had set up a buffet of sandwiches and salads for them, courtesy of her friend Travis, who owned his own catering company. If it was a true example of his work, his food was delicious. He must get a lot of business from her, and rightly so. Kiley ate a warm turkey sandwich with only cheese and honey mustard sauce. It had more flavor than she knew it could have.

"Oh, the baby is getting so big. Jane, you must be an excellent mother," their mom said as she could not take her eyes off of him. Ethan played quietly on a blanket on the floor. A blue, striped giraffe was holding his attention. Jane bent over every so often and wound it up, so that it would play "Twinkle, Twinkle, Little Star" for him.

Their mother was wearing an old, worn dress. It was one Kiley remembered her mother wearing when she was still in high school. Maybe she should take pity on her mom and do a mother-daughter shopping day with her sometime. Then Kiley thought of all the awkward silences they would have to fill, all the questions her mother would ask Kiley about her life that she wouldn't want to answer, and thought better of it.

"Ethan does all the work... And Kiley helps too," Jane added. She wasn't accustomed to receiving compliments from her mother, and it showed.

"YOU help with the baby?" Miley snorted.

"Yes, I live in the same house. He is right across the hall, so it really isn't that hard."

"So, you like, just sit around and play with the baby all day? Isn't that kind of boring?" Miley probed Kiley.

"No, I am writing my next book. It is going to have much more action than my first one," she stated proudly.

"Does it still have a fairy tale theme?" Miley asked.

"No. And you know that was just an accident the first time," Kiley pouted.

"That still doesn't seem like enough stuff to keep you busy for six months," Miley pushed. Her sister knew Kiley too well.

"Well, I have started seeing a guy...," Kiley began.

"OMG! Dish! Tell me everything."

Miley seemed to have forgotten that their mother was in the room. There would be limited juicy details given in her presence.

"Now?" Jane mouthed to Kiley, but she kept going.

"Ya. He is a great guy," Kiley said.

"So he's local? Do we know him?" Miley pushed excitedly.

You walked with him at Jane's wedding, Kiley thought.

"It's funny, but you sorta do. But he is so much nicer and funnier and sweeter than his reputation...," Kiley said, trying to lay some good groundwork, but feeling as if she was digging a bigger hole for herself instead.

"Ooo. A bad boy. But I thought Jane got the last one," Miley said.

"Um" was all Kiley could reply.

Jane coughed loudly, a hysterical laugh catching in her throat.

"What? Who is it?" Miley caught on, looking back and forth between her sisters.

"Who is the biggest bad boy left in that town?" When no response came, Miley spoke again. She began naming random names of boys they went to school with. "Mark Malone? John Travis. Billy Eastman? Wait, he wasn't bad... Oh! Who was the kid who set fire to the high school?"

"Josh Tucker," Jane chirped, then covered her laughing mouth.

"Oh My God! Josh Tucker!" Miley shouted, training her steely tawny eyes on Kiley.

"Hey, in his defense, that was all Wade's fault!" Kiley yelled, pointing to Jane, who was now rolling around on the floor laughing. She was laughing so hard, she didn't get a chance to defend Wade's honor. Seeing his mom in such a state upset Ethan, who began to cry. His grandmother picked him up from the floor and cradled him to her chest.

"Is this SERIOUS?" Miley asked Kiley.

"Ya, I think so," Kiley said, suddenly unsure under her twin sister's judgmental glare.

"Jane?" Miley moved her stare to Jane for a more impartial opinion.

"Yes, definitely," Jane answered.

"God, Kiley. I thought you were smarter than that!" Miley exclaimed.

"What do you mean by that? You don't even know him!" she shouted angrily. Kiley found it ironic that Miley had teased her about liking Josh at the hospital when Ethan had been born, before Kiley had even started anything with him. Miley was all onboard, as long as it was all just a big joke. She apparently never saw Josh as boyfriend material, especially for her twin sister. Miley and Kiley had been so alike for the first fourteen years of their lives that it was like they had been the same person. It was like Miley had never gotten over the fact that that was no longer the case.

"I know you could do better. What happened to Ted?" Miley asked accusingly.

"I dropped his ass," she replied.

"Kiley, language," her mother scolded.

"That must be Josh's influence," Miley stated sarcastically.

"No, it's ME. Ted was just a hanger-on. He was only with me because of my book. I don't even think he ever loved me."

"Sometimes you have to do the sensible thing, not what feels right for the moment," Miley lectured.

"Oh, so I should have a dysfunctional relationship like you and Sandy."

"Leave Sandy out of this!" Miley raised her voice.

"He is just using you for a place to live. Half the time he brings other girls home, right in front of you. Is that what you call love?"

"Sandy's a lesbian?" their mom asked, confusion crossing her face. No one heard her.

"Kiley, you don't understand our relationship..."

"I know that you will never be happy living like that."

"Wait, Sandy's a man?" their mom interjected. They ignored her.

"I have lived my life looking for love. It's not like we grew up with a lot of it. I'm not just going to throw it aside when I find it because you don't approve." Kiley was glad she had stood up for herself and told her sister how she really felt.

She just didn't understand why her sister had such a horrified expression on her face. Had what Kiley said been meaner than she intended? Had Kiley said something she didn't mean to? A look at Jane's face made that an affirmative.

Kiley rewound her previous sentences in her head like an analog cassette tape.

■　▶▶　■　◀

STOP. REWIND. STOP. PLAY.

'It's not like we grew up with a lot of it.'

Oops. That would be the inappropriate statement. In itself, it wasn't a bad remark. Kiley and her sisters made comments like that all the time among themselves. But the faux pas was in saying it in front of their mother. It would probably hurt her feelings. But more than that, they just didn't discuss deep feelings, or feelings at all, with their mother. They didn't talk about anything "real" with their parents. It seemed like it would open up a Pandora's box that no one really wanted to explore. Their complaining gave them a release, without actually having to confront the problems causing their family discord.

"Oh, God. I'm sorry, Mom. I didn't mean anything by that. I was just—," Kiley backpedaled.

"It's fine. I know what you are saying," she replied.

"But I shouldn't have said it," Kiley begged.

"You can always say what you want to. I am not made of glass. I won't break."

There was an uncomfortable pause in the room while everyone waited for each other to change the subject. No one did. Baby Ethan had regained his good mood. He gurgled and giggled in his grandmother's arms.

"I believe I owe you all a long-overdue explanation," their mom said. No one made a sound. Their mother was so quiet that no one even knew if she was going to finish her own statement. But they were all very intrigued.

"Your father and I had a lot of love to share when we got married. In looking back, I can see that we should have loved each other more. We liked each other, but we were never in the kind of love you see in a movie, read in books..." Mrs. Riley gave Kiley a loving glance.

"With all this extra love, we wanted to give it to a baby. What none of you know is that we had that baby. And your father and I loved that baby very much. But it started having problems right away and the doctors told us the baby had a hole in its heart. Shortly after that, the baby passed away." Tears spilled down Mrs. Riley's face as she finished her story, staring down at little Ethan. Kiley thought she was done, but she went on.

"That loss cast a shadow over our marriage that never went away. Our marriage seemed empty. Having another child of our own seemed too painful, so we adopted." She now nodded to Jane, who was also crying. "Then we had the pleasant surprise of you girls three years later."

"I thought you adopted me because you couldn't have kids," Jane stated.

"Oh, I knew that is what you thought, but I never told you that," she said.

"How could you lose a baby, and no one in Oakley ever mentioned it?" Miley asked, always concentrating on the gossip.

"Because then we lived in Huntington. We moved to Oakley when your father got a job with the accountant that already had an office there... I'm sorry that our house was never overflowing with love. We realized this, but we didn't know how to change it. We tried to make it up to you girls by being extra supportive. It probably wasn't the best method, but it was all we had. Maybe if your father and I had divorced sooner, you would have grown up with a different experience. We will never know."

"Why didn't you ever tell us?" Kiley asked.

"Oh, I don't know. It was too soon afterwards. Then it was too personal, too painful. Then it didn't seem like details you girls needed to know. But maybe it would have made your growing up environment make more sense. We will never know."

"Well, thank you for finally telling us," Jane consoled her.

"Is there any chance my heart could be holey?" Miley asked.

"Oh no, sweetie. They checked you and your sister out for that when you were born."

"They should have checked your brain too," Kiley said to her twin. Miley even managed to make a story about a dead baby about her.

"They should have checked YOUR head. You are the one dating Josh Tucker. Seriously?" Miley asked.

"Seriously," Kiley answered.

"He isn't even that handsome. And his clothes are always so rumpled. And he looks like he doesn't even own a razor," Miley prattled on.

"And he is a great lover. And he loves me," Kiley replied, not caring anymore that her mother was in the room listening. It seemed like all the other half-truths and evasions had been thrown out the window today, why not a few more?

"Well, you will excuse me if I need to vet him myself before I believe that," Miley said.

"Come over anytime," Kiley offered.

"I'll be there tomorrow then."

"We are moving furniture tomorrow. But you are welcome to join the moving party."

"Next week, perhaps... Josh Tucker. You know, you could have just started dating him years ago, if you were going to choose someone so close to home."

"Eh, he wasn't ready for me years ago. But he is now."

"Now Miley, about your roommate Sandy…," their mother began.

EPILOGUE

Kiley and Josh were slumped on the couch in the Tucker living room, flipping through the TV channels. They had helped Jane and Wade move into their house today. Not everything had gotten moved, but the bed and the crib had, so they were spending the night there for the first time.

Pete and Mackenzie were due to move into their new house next week. They would all be in excellent physical shape after all the heavy lifting was said and done. It was strange to not hear the baby crying in the house.

"So, what are you going to do now?" Josh asked Kiley.

"About what?" Kiley asked.

"Where will you stay? Will you go live with Jane, or stay in the room next to me for easy access lovin'?" Josh smiled wide, his white teeth gleaming at her.

"I was kind of hoping you would make an honest woman out of me someday. Give me a last name that doesn't rhyme with my first name."

Josh raised an eyebrow. "Hey now, we have only officially been going out for like two weeks."

"I've found what I want. Why wait? You sure aren't getting any younger," she chided him, poking him in the ribs with her finger.

"But having a 22-year-old girlfriend is way hotter than having a 22-year-old-wife," Josh explained.

"Hmmm. In that case, maybe I'll move to New York. Or L.A."

"You don't have the money for that," he grumbled dismissively, looking back to the television.

"Oh, I forgot to tell you. While you guys were out at the Diner for lunch, I got a phone call. Plateau Studios wants to option the rights to my book to make a movie. Their offer is big enough I could pay for an apartment. And buy a few furnishings from Ikea," Kiley said.

"You're kidding," Josh said, his mouth hanging open in surprise.

"No. You think my cheesy young adult book isn't good enough to be made into a cheesy young adult movie?" Kiley looked at him, her bottom lip thrust out into a pout.

"No, not at all. I just can't believe you didn't fuckin' tell me this sooner! This is huge!" He jumped up, and then picked her up and spun her around, kissing her in the process. "I'm so proud of you, baby."

"I never thought of myself as anyone's 'baby,' " Kiley said, scrunching up her nose.

"It felt like a 'baby' kind of moment," he told her.

"OK. I'll buy that," Kiley said. They both sat back down and returned to their couch potato positions, as if huge news had not just been revealed.

"When does it all get finalized?"

"Probably in the next few weeks. My lawyer is looking at it now," Kiley answered.

"YOU have a lawyer?" he asked.

"Sure. Mr. Drexel."

"The only lawyer in Oakley? The one your mom, and now Mackenzie, work for? What does he know about movie contracts?"

"Probably not much. But at least he can understand the lawyer speak, which is more than I can do."

Kiley flipped past some gymnastics event on TV, then flipped back.

"Hey, I wonder if Ted's new girlfriend is competing," Kiley said.

"Why do you care?"

"Morbid curiosity."

"Do you remember her name?"

"Tiffany, with way too many extra letters," Kiley replied.

"I think they are only giving their last names," Josh said, skeptically.

"Oh my God, that is her!" The camera was on a girl in a leotard with her hair pulled up into a bun, preparing to begin her routine. The shot cut to the stands, where her parents sat proudly. But, who was that guy sitting next to them with the black eye and busted nose?

"Oh my God! There's Ted. But what's wrong with his face?" Kiley squinted at the screen for answers.

"You called him right. What a groupie." Josh's casual reply was meant to be a cover. But, instead, it gave him away. Or maybe he didn't care.

"Oh my God! Your sore hand you were complaining about today—you went and bet up Ted!" Kiley accused.

"And I would totally do it again. He didn't do right by you. That guy is King of the Weasels. Someone had to teach him you don't treat Kiley Riley-Tucker like that."

"Oh, how could you? You left in the rhyme."

"Are you mad at me?" Josh asked sheepishly.

"No. I should be. But I'm actually kind of turned on," Kiley said. She gave him a sly smile. She forgot for a moment that she never gave full tooth smiles, because they showed off her crooked tooth.

"Really?"

"Maybe you should come act as my security guard for my next book tour."

"That sounds like you want to watch me pound people."

"Only when it's necessary. I just spent yesterday trying to convince my family that you were a 'reformed' bad boy," Kiley said.

"Ya, that's the day I went up to Fredrickstown and set him straight."

"My hero."

"I'm trouble. I am just wise enough with age to keep it on the down low," Josh admitted.

"I knew you were trouble when I walked in."

"Ya, I get that a lot," Josh responded coyly.

"You better not get that anymore, from anyone other than me!" Kiley playfully punched him, but Josh took the opportunity to tackle her on the couch and make out with her. Kiley put her arms around Josh and kissed him, knowing she would never let him go. Going forward, she and Josh and Dave would be their own little family.

Just then Evan and Donna entered the room, coughing and making loud scuffling noises, leaving Josh and Kiley no choice but to uncouple from one another.

JOSH

"I have a surprise for you," Kiley whispered into Josh's ear, as they headed upstairs, away from prying parental eyes.

"Ya, what's that?" Josh asked, curious.

"When I was at my mother's house, I found a little something you might be interested in," she cooed, leading him to her bedroom and opening the door for them both.

"This isn't like an old yearbook or something, is it? Because I wasn't always the handsome devil that you know now," he stuttered, worried.

"I believe you once requested to see me in this..." Kiley sat a cardboard box on her bed, and pulled out a red and white uniform. She held it up in front of her and did a little shimmy dance. It was very obviously two sizes too small for her fully-grown adult figure. But that made Josh that much more eager to see her put it on.

"You know, J.K., I usually don't feel old, but seeing you in that outfit might just give me a heart attack."

"Does that mean that you want me to pack it away again, inside this dark little box, never to see the light of day?" she asked in a high-pitched, baby doll voice.

"Oh no, I'm not saying that. I am saying it will be totally worth seeing you wear it even if the worst should happen."

Kiley took her shirt off, and stood next to her bed in only her bra, which happened to be red as well. She must have planned it that way.

"I will wear this uniform for you. I may even shake my pompoms for you. But on one condition," Kiley proposed, holding the cheerleading sweater up again in front of her.

"Anything." As soon as it escaped Josh's mouth, he knew it was the truth. He WOULD do anything for her, uniform or no uniform, until the end of time. But admitting it so openly to her so soon could very easily end up biting him in the ass.

"Stop calling me J.K. Stop calling me any names that are not mine."

"That's a deal," he said, exhaling. This request he found very reasonable. She could have asked for so many other things from him.

"I'm glad that we aren't going to have a problem with that," she said, slipping the sweater over her head. The roundness of the top of her breasts was on display, as well as a thick width of her pale stomach.

"Now show me that skirt and those pompoms, sugar."

"Oh, you are so going to get it!"

"I sure hope so."

In the third book of The Riley Sisters series—

Miley Riley always dreamed of being famous in the spotlights of Hollywood. Achieving those dreams seemed pretty unlikely coming from the Podunk farm town of Oakley, Alabama. With no talents and no college education, she had settled into her career as a party planner and sharing an apartment with her on-again, off-again boyfriend. When the movie based on her twin sister Kiley's book begins shooting in California, Miley wastes no time in making the trip with her for a once in a lifetime vacation. Her wildest fantasies come true when she meets a dark-haired heartthrob, rising movie star Mark Tennyson. Their relationship heats up quickly, much to the chagrin of Miley's family and best friend Travis.

When her new L.A. life begins to publicly crumble, Miley discovers who she can really count on. The road back to her real life returns her to Alabama, but will be filled with unconventional risks. Miley will learn to *Be Careful What You Wish For*...

BE CAREFUL WHAT YOU WISH FOR

JANUARY 2016

Find out how it all began—

JENNIFER FRIESS is an author, blogger, and editor who lives in Lenawee County, Michigan, with her husband, son, and dog. She loves entertainment trivia. She doesn't match her socks. She is a picky eater and likes it that way. In addition to *When You Least Expect It*, Jennifer has previously published *The Wind Could Blow a Bug*, the first book in The Riley Sisters series.

Follow Jennifer here:

BLOG: ImNotStalkingYou.com
My mildly entertaining random thoughts

TWITTER: @jenf2

FACEBOOK: www.facebook.com/imnotstalkingyou2